Learning from Loss

Learning from Loss

Lessons from Our Gurus

Renuka Narayanan

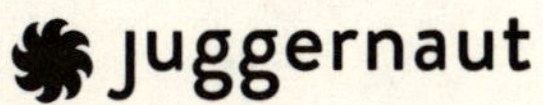

JUGGERNAUT BOOKS
C-I-128, First Floor, Sangam Vihar, Near Holi Chowk,
New Delhi 110080, India

First published by Juggernaut Books 2022

10 9 8 7 6 5 4 3 2 1

PISBN: 9789393986375
EISBN: 9789393986382

Typeset in Adobe Caslon Pro by
R. Ajith Kumar, Noida

Printed at Thomson Press India Ltd

To the storytellers of India who continue to enchant and inspire

I see myself as joined to their tradition, particularly to the free-ranging and interpretative oral tradition of Harikatha, or devotional discourse, popular in many Indian languages.

Contents

Introduction

Grief comes in many guises and puts us on a painful personal journey that we must walk alone. There are many sentimental and philosophical sayings about loss and grief, but there is no getting around the fact that it hurts. Grief leaves us in tears, shed or unshed, and robs us of sleep and laughter. It can discourage us so much that we are unable to function normally. Learning from loss is a slow struggle. Different people react in different ways and take their own time to deal with it.

Indeed, we are frequently told that time heals, but not how long it takes. That seems to depend on our individual sadhana, or emotional practice. There are no rules, nor is it in the least dishonourable to grieve. Being human, we cannot help but mourn our loss. But beyond the dark shadow of grief lies the golden calm of peace if we let our hearts and minds take us forward into it.

Our Indian stories have a great deal to offer us on coping with loss and grief. In my view, the epics and the lives and parables of saints and sages are principally about anger management and recovery from loss. They are like an illustrative textbook on response options. Somebody loses a loved one, somebody loses his honour, somebody feels abandoned by fate and deserted by luck. In selecting these stories, I looked for a variety of causes and responses across time and space from classical Hindu, Buddhist and Bhakti traditions. These stories touched a deep chord in me as I hope they will in you. I wish each one of us success in our personal journeys.

1

Living with Loss

How do you live with the loss of your loved ones, one after the other? This ancient story of Devahuti's brave effort to cope is found in the early chapters of the Bhagavata Purana or Srimad Bhagavatam, one of the holiest books in the Hindu tradition, at par with the two epics, the Ramayana and the Mahabharata. The Bhagavatam is important to all three major schools of Hindu philosophy, Advaita, Vishishta-Advaita and Dvaita. Attributed to Veda Vyasa, it is said to have been composed after the Mahabharata and was imparted to King Parikshit in the last week of his life by Shuka, Vyasa's son.

'You must choose the colours you like for your trousseau,' said Shatarupa to her daughter Devahuti, turning over a heap of silks. 'There is nothing that your father cannot get for you.'

'But mother, you are marrying me to a hermit. Will I need such clothes in his ashram?'

'Devahuti, you chose him yourself. These clothes will only add to your beauty as a bride. Don't refuse me,' said Shatarupa with a note of anxiety creeping in, for Devahuti was every bit as determined and passionate in her convictions as her father, Manu, the lord of the earthly world.

'Very well!' said Devahuti in laughing submission and began to put aside shades of blue silk that would set off her own deep blue eyes. Delicately built, with long black hair, she wondered what her husband-to-be actually looked like.

Devahuti had never set eyes on him. But Narada, the wandering sage, who went about the three worlds minding everybody's business, had often told her about the bright young hermit, Kardama, who lived by the banks of the holy river Sarasvati. According to Narada, Kardama was muscular, strong and handsome, besides being endowed with a ferocious intellect. 'He is a lion of a man,' declared Narada. 'I am almost afraid to visit him because he glows with such lustre that I fear my eyes will dim.'

Devahuti's interest had been fairly caught and she found herself wondering more and more about Kardama. When her parents told her that they wanted to get her married, she said boldly that she would like to marry Kardama.

A curious thing had then come to pass. Kardama – who had completed his days as a student and now lived alone in his hut by the river – lost in meditation, had prayed to Lord Narayana, the Almighty. 'Please find me a suitable wife, Lord,' he had prayed. 'I wish to move to the next stage of life as a householder, and once I complete that duty, I wish to take sanyas and think only of you, with total concentration.'

Lord Narayana was very pleased with Kardama's resolute aim and told him in a dream that Devahuti, a daughter of Manu and Shatarupa, king and queen of the world, would be his bride.

He also informed Manu, in a dream, that it was his wish that Devahuti should marry Kardama, a son, like Manu, of Lord Brahma. Thus, Devahuti's marriage was made in heaven itself, and in two days, she would be taken to Kardama by her parents.

~

As Kardama sat by the rippling Sarasvati, he saw the royal procession approaching his hut and went to greet it. Devahuti and Kardama looked at each other, and it's safe to say that they fell instantly in love. Kardama was as manly and handsome as Sage Narada had described, and Devahuti looked like Mahalakshmi incarnate in her silk-clad beauty with pearls and flowers woven in her hair. Nevertheless, Kardama had reservations.

'O king! You are a great and just ruler of whom everyone speaks well. You are the son of Lord Brahma himself, who created this world and all mankind. You are wealthy like no other. How will the princess cope with my simple, hard existence and all the fasts and austerities that my wife will have to undertake as part of my religious life?'

'She has chosen you herself, and Lord Narayana himself has promised her to you,' said Manu, embarrassed by Kardama's praise.

'I have another point to raise. I prayed to Lord Narayana to find me a suitable wife, but I also said I would leave the householder's life after my children were born. Will the princess accept this? Will you?'

Devahuti looked again at Kardama, and before she knew it, her head nodded. Her parents' consent was a mere formality after that determined nod.

Devahuti and Kardama were married without further ado around the fire, and Lord Brahma himself came by to bless his son and granddaughter.

After her parents left her to her new life as Kardama's wife, Devahuti's first move was to tidily put away her bridal finery and dress herself in the simple garments suited to forest life.

~

Years passed by with Devahuti serving Kardama, as Parvati did Shiva, during his meditation. One day, as Devahuti approached him carrying a pot of water from the river with her customary cheerful smile, Kardama took a good look at her. Where had his fairy-tale bride vanished without a sound of protest? Devahuti's limbs had grown painfully thin because of her never-ending austerities. Her long hair was twisted into a severe, practical knot. Her blue eyes had dimmed in lustre from years of fasting. Her face looked pinched although it smiled as sweetly as it had that first morning. She had long ago given away all her finery to visitors and villagers and was dressed in coarse, plain cloth.

'Dear wife, we have been lost in my austerities, have we not? But I never heard you complain,' said Kardama tenderly. 'Is there anything I can do to please you?'

'I would like to have children', said Devahuti in her direct, straightforward way, her spirit undimmed by her choice to live the hard life. A vague sense of unease crossed her mind at that moment but she could not think why and smiled instead at Kardama, who looked steadily back at her.

'Why don't you put that pot down and bathe in the river? I will wait for you,' said Kardama gently at last.

Devahuti did so, and as she emerged she was greatly astonished by the change in her. Her skin felt smooth and tight, her limbs were shapely and rounded, her rustic garments had changed to silk, and her hair flowed long and silken to her knees as before.

Devahuti understood, at once, that it was Kardama's yogic power that had wrought the transformation. At the door of their hut stood a magic chariot with wings, a vimana, and Kardama, looking fresh, young and handsome, stood by it, holding out his hand. Devahuti happily put her hand in his.

A long, enchanted honeymoon followed, and nine

beautiful daughters were born to them over the years. Devahuti revelled in being a mother, and Kardama was a loving, liberal father who taught his girls to read and write. Both parents taught them the life skills needed in an ashram, from collecting food to cooking it, from fetching wood to making fires, from drawing water to weaving mats and growing flowers for worship. They were a large, happy family living peacefully by the banks of the Sarasvati without a care in the world.

But one day, Lord Brahma came to visit along with nine tough young hermits, each with rippling muscles, a body hardened to iron by austerities and a broad forehead glowing with intelligence. 'My children, you are an exemplary family,' he said to Kardama and Devahuti. 'You have led clean, good lives and your daughters have been raised to be intelligent and good-natured. Marry them now to these bridegrooms of my choice so that they may go out and found their own families.'

Devahuti and Kardama did not wish to be parted from their daughters. But the world was young then, and they did not know many people for there were not that many people inhabiting the land those days. Accepting Lord Brahma's grandfatherly interest, they made the young hermits welcome and prepared their daughters with loving words of reassurance and advice. Kala was married to Marichi, Anasuya to Atri, Shraddha to Angiras, Havirbhu to Pulastya, Gati to Pulaha, Kriya to Kratu, Khyati to Brighu, Arundhati to Vashishta, and the youngest daughter, Shanti, to Atharva.

The sacred fire bore witness to their weddings, and each daughter was given a cloth bundle of hastily collected things to start domestic life with.

The newly-weds were duly seen off, with Kardama and Devahuti bravely holding back their tears.

~

Devahuti felt extremely lonely without her daughters and moped about the house for days. Her home felt bereft and empty. She rallied herself that the empty nest was in the natural order of things. However, she went about her household duties with a heavy heart, missing her children very much.

But a new and even more terrible blow was to fall. Not much longer after the girls had departed, leaving the little hermitage morosely silent, Kardama sat Devahuti down and told her his plans. 'Devahuti, I told you about this before we were married. I have completed my duties as a householder now, and I must go away for good as a renunciate, a sanyasi. I am going far away and will never see you again.'

Devahuti's long habit of uncomplaining cheerfulness broke at this thunderclap. She dissolved in angry tears. 'I have spent my whole life devoted to you. And I am expecting our tenth child. How can you leave me like this?'

'Devahuti, please understand. Your child will be a son; he will be Lord Narayana's gift to you. I have no fears for his future.'

After a pause, Devahuti said sadly, 'I love you. You are the sum and substance of my life. How unlucky am I that I have been deceived by the Lord's maya. I am afraid of this world, afraid of losing you, afraid of what will happen. What should I do?'

'I love you too, but I must go. Pray to Lord Narayana. He will show you the way, don't be afraid,' said Kardama, and before she knew it, he was gone. Just like that, after years of a close, happy marriage and warm family life, Devahuti's husband vanished forever in pursuit of his own goals. Her girlish dreams of happiness, her womanly yearnings, counted as nothing.

~

Kardama went miles away, deep into the forest. Embraced by the woods, he felt cut off from all attachment. His mind, body and spirit seemed to fuse gradually into a harmony of being that was powerfully unlike anything he had felt before. Sitting in yogic silence, in love with his breath – which he controlled more and more – his days slid by like an uninterrupted dream in which he thought only of God. One golden morning, in this state of transcendent calm, his breath stopped, and he felt his spirit disappear into the light that was the Lord.

~

Devahuti, meanwhile, struggled alone at home, awaiting the birth of her child, helped by an attendant that her grieving mother, Shatarupa, sent her. Eventually, a beautiful boy was born to Devahuti, whom she named Kapila. Lost in thoughts of Kardama, she looked after her son with the automatic knack of years of motherhood, but her heart was not in it. Occasionally, she caught her son in her arms and wept over his soft curls, remembering Kardama and her daughters.

A new period of loneliness commenced when Kapila was old enough to be sent to gurukul, to a preceptor some distance away. After that, Devahuti sent her attendant back to Shatarupa for she wanted to brood alone.

She took Kardama's parting words to heart and determinedly prayed to Lord Narayana as she went about her daily tasks, fetching wood and water, gathering fruit, nuts and herbs, cooking her simple meals. She fell asleep exhausted every night, having kept herself busy the whole day in an effort to pass time meaningfully. Her heart felt broken and her mind was never calm, for her disturbed thoughts of loss and her fears about the future did not let her enjoy any peace despite her prayers and fasts.

But one day, Kapila came back home.

'Are your studies completed, my son?' asked Devahuti, after blessing him in welcome.

'Yes, dear Mother, I am home now.' Kapila smiled, holding her hand.

Devahuti flew to her household tasks with her old spring,

humming happily as she did everything she could to make Kapila comfortable. She cooked his favourite gruel of boiled millet flavoured with wild ginger, wild turmeric and tender greens. How tall he had grown, how very much he resembled both his father and her. She could not take her eyes off him. That day, she prayed to Lord Narayana in blissful gratitude and slept peacefully.

But the very next morning, her old anxieties began to devour her again. 'I am afraid of losing him next,' she warned herself, but the worry ate her up all the same. Seeing her unhappy face, Kapila asked her what troubled her.

His anxious face was a jolt to Devahuti. She fetched a small pot of water and drank a little to steady herself. 'It is time I faced up to the reality of existence but I still don't know how,' she told herself. 'My husband told me that Lord Narayana would help me fight my fears. Here is my son, radiant with good thoughts and deep learning. He is the Almighty's gift to me. Perhaps Lord Narayana will speak to me through him.'

Some of her old determination came back and she turned her anxious face to look at Kapila. She said, 'My dear son, I need your help. I have always been clear in my choices. But my attachment to you all has turned into a thorn in my heart. I am miserable about losing your father and your sisters. And now I am afraid to lose you. Set me free from this terrible anxiety, my son. How may I be at peace and break these bonds like your father set out to do? I am unused to going alone into the deep forest. I need to learn to be at peace here, at home. Please won't you tell me how?'

'Mother, I noticed that you keep busy all day long. The house and garden are spotless. The puja flowers grow in profusion ... the malli, the bakula, the champaka, the arali, beloved of Shiva, the tulsi we offer Lord Narayana. The grain jars are full, and there is a good store of freshly husked paddy. This shelf is loaded with pots of all the pickles, chutneys and preserves you have made ... wild berry, lemon, mango, brinjal and pumpkin. You are tireless in body, yet your soul is crushed, Mother.'

'Of what use is my life, son, without my husband?'

'Mother, it's not like that! You chose your life; you have been happy. Nothing lasts forever, Mother. It is the nature of human life.'

'I have never complained until the day your father went away. And then, I was so overwhelmed by my loss that I was embarrassed to ask for help. Nor did I know whom to ask. But now I feel there is no shame in asking someone of good mind who has studied these things. You have learnt Brahma Vidya, the knowledge of existence, have you not? Now please impart it to me, my son.'

Kapila smiled at his mother with affection and respect.

'Mother, I will gladly tell you. It is so easy that anyone can understand. It is the mind, Mother, that is the cause of both bondage and freedom. Experience is made of three gunas, or qualities, of peace, involvement and negativity. They are called sattva, rajas and tamas. When the balance of these gunas is disturbed, emotions take over and cause unhappiness. The mind turns away from its contemplative inner self and is locked in a weary battle with every passing emotion. So far, the surest way out known to man is the remedial path of bhakti.'

'I have prayed and fasted so much, my son, but it has not helped me.'

'Mother, bhakti, or devotion, is a gradual process. The mind will not cooperate at first because the hold of the world is so strong. Think more and more of the Lord, Mother, until it takes over your mind and frees it from worldly attachments. Sanga is the state of attachment. Mukta Sanga is freedom from attachment. Attachment to God loosens the bonds of other attachments, slowly but surely.'

'How may I help that process, son?'

'Mother, read and listen to stories about God, hear and sing songs about God, be gentle to all you meet, which you are anyway, for the Lord loves kind words and deeds and a lack of anger and greed. We are basically afraid of Time, Mother, which gives and takes away from human life. But when we realize that God is Time, we find perspective. These gains and losses are inevitable and mean less and less when we make God our one true and constant friend.'

'It is cold comfort to me in my grief, son, but there seems to be no other way out,' said Devahuti.

Nevertheless, she thanked her son for his guidance and went to sit by the river to think his words over. As she knew instinctively that he would, Kapila, too, went away soon after. He travelled north-west where he found a peaceful forest to retire in. But his earthly mission was done. His teachings to his mother, which she shared with all who came her way thereafter, and spread widely, came to be known as Sankhya philosophy. Meanwhile, Devahuti's daughters propagated the human race, and so Kardama became known as 'Kardama Prajapati', an ancestor of mankind.

Devahuti lived on alone at the hermitage that had been her home for so many years. She never stopped missing her family and struggled bravely to find the peace her son had described. She practised yoga, lived an even simpler life, prayed and meditated sincerely. She cried very often at first, but the weeping bouts reduced over time. 'Everything comes from Time, and Time is God, so why be disturbed?' she told herself repeatedly. As the years rolled by, Devahuti tried very hard to throw herself into endless activity to distract herself from the loss of everything she held dear.

Bit by bit, as Kapila had promised, she reached a stage of mental calm after some years where she felt neither glad nor sad. Instead, she felt a peace that seemed much better than the agitation of love and nowhere as chaotic as the loss by which she was tormented when Kardama went away. When it was time for her breath to cease, Devahuti went quietly to her refuge in the Lord, her mind as limpid as the waters of the holy Sarasvati.

2

Looking for Love

Could you bear it if you were rejected by your own father? The haunting story of Dhruva, the child seeker, is found in great detail in the Vishnu Purana and in the Bhagavata Purana, also known as the Srimad Bhagavatam, attributed to Veda Vyasa, the composer of the Mahabharata. Dhruva's all-too-human plight and extraordinary attempt to win love have been retold in many regional Indian cultures across time, in books and in the visual and performing arts. This retelling is joined to the Harikatha, the devotional storytelling tradition still hugely popular in India in various languages.

Dhruva was only five, but what a bright, determined five-year-old he was. His gentle mother, Suniti, had a difficult time keeping up with his adventurous spirit and his cuts and grazes from play. Nor would Dhruva listen when summoned down from a tree too high for a five-year-old to climb.

'I can do it. Watch me!' he would cry from a perilously slanted branch, gather himself tightly and leap safely to the ground ten feet below.

Suniti was both worried about his safety and pleased with his boldness. After all, Dhruva was the eldest son of King Uttanapada and would be king one day. That was his right. But Suniti had grown unsure about Dhruva's future ever since the king had married a younger girl, Suruchi. The new bride had completely cast a spell on the king, who made his preference painfully obvious to Suniti.

Suniti was now the classic neglected wife, while Suruchi and her young son, Uttama, were the king's favourites. Dhruva was too young to understand, since he was busy with a hundred childish schemes for play. He barely noticed that his father no longer came to his mother's apartments or that his mother looked downcast all the time. She never cried in Dhruva's presence, but she laughed less and less.

One fine morning, Dhruva spotted his father playing in the garden with Uttama and bounded joyously towards them. The king was sitting on a bench and had just picked up Uttama to cuddle him. Dhruva ran up to them and tried to climb on to his father's lap, saying, 'Father! Hold me, too!'

But Uttama's mother, Suruchi, was nearby, and she pounced on Dhruva. Wrenching his little arm, she angrily dragged him off the bench.

'Wretched boy, you cannot sit on the king's lap. You are not my son! Pray to Lord Narayana to be born my son in your next birth!'

The king was so besotted with Suruchi that he said nothing.

Dhruva's face crumpled. He looked pitifully at his father, but he got no response, and his eyes filled with tears.

'Won't you hold me, Father?' he asked, his voice trembling. But Uttanapada refused to speak a word or make a sign. Dhruva choked on a sob at this utter rejection and ran away as fast as his legs could carry him to his mother's apartment.

Suniti rushed to hug the weeping Dhruva when he burst into her room.

'Dear son, what is the matter?' she asked in her gentle way.

When Dhruva sobbed out the story, Suniti felt helpless against her circumstances as a powerless, rejected wife.

'Perhaps she is right, son. Pray to Lord Narayana to make you feel better.'

'Mother, I want my father to love me. Can Lord Narayana make that happen'?

'He can do anything, son. Both the common people and the great saints and sages who worship him in the forest believe it.'

Suniti meant only to console Dhruva and was unprepared for the fierce spark that lit in his eyes at that.

'I will find him then, and make him listen to me,' he said, with childish resolution. 'I want to be the highest person in the world whom nobody can pull down. Father will have to love me then.'

'You are too little to go into the forest, son. You will feel better after some time,' said Suniti consolingly, but Dhruva did not reply. Suniti tried to hold him back, but he disappeared into his room and Suniti let him go, thinking that he was tired by the emotional upset and wanted to rest.

But two hours later, when she went to wake him up, she found that Dhruva had disappeared. After looking for him all over the place, Suniti thought of questioning the palace guards and was horrified to learn that Dhruva had walked out alone through the gates and had not returned.

~

Dhruva trudged on resolutely through the streets, asking passers-by the way to the forest. Though they were surprised to see such a small boy out alone, he wore such a purposeful look on his face that nobody thought to deny him an answer to his quick, curt questions.

In less than three hours, Dhruva found himself at the edge of the forest and marched boldly into it, finding jungle tracks as he went along. His head felt light with fatigue, and his heart felt heavy with misery. He was propelled forward, unafraid by his deep anger and impatiently brushed aside the low branches in his path, occasionally wincing as thorns pricked his feet or scratched his arms.

The light began to fade and, feeling thirsty, he stopped by a little stream and cupped his hands to drink the water. He sat down by the stream to rest a little and to choose his direction.

'Narayana! Narayana!' said an astonished voice suddenly. Dhruva whipped around to see a holy man carrying a lute who had appeared out of the forest.

Dhruva's training made him scramble to his feet at once and offer a namaste to the sage, whose eyes softened.

'What are you doing alone in the forest, child?' said the sage.

Dhruva told him his story in a tired little voice; he was barely able to speak.

Telling Dhruva to sit down again, the sage introduced himself.

'I am Narada, who roams the three realms. Long, long ago, I was a small boy like you, wandering about the world, alone. Listen to me, dear child. You are too young to let insults upset you so deeply. You are only five years old. Your place is by your mother's side, playing with your toys and learning your letters. Your mother may have told you to pray to Lord Narayana. But, child, do you know how hard it is to find him? Rishis and yogis have spent their whole lives looking for him. It takes hard work to please him. Go home in peace, and let your life work itself out. Your mother must be anxious.'

Dhruva shook his head stubbornly.

'Thank you for telling me this. But I will and shall find Lord Narayana. Please teach me how to find him. Please.'

Narada was perplexed. It was clearly his duty to take the boy home. But what a fire blazed in his young eyes. Narada remembered his own lonely quest for the Lord, as an orphan in his last birth. His heart went out to Dhruva, and he resolved to help him.

'Very well, my child. I will take you to a forest by the banks of the river Yamuna. It is called Madhuvan, the honey forest. It is said that Lord Narayana may always be found by the Yamuna, and that Madhuvan is a place especially dear to him. I will tell you what to do when we get there. Eat these berries that I have kept knotted in my cloth. Let us sleep here tonight, for you must be exhausted.'

~

The next morning, Sage Narada, by his yogic powers, airlifted Dhruva to Madhuvan. It took place in the blink of an eye before Dhruva even knew what was happening.

'Now choose a tree to sit under, and I will tell you the next step,' said Narada. Dhruva looked around and chose a fine, big pipal.

'After I leave, sit cross-legged with your hands on your knees, shut your eyes and keep absolutely still. Picture Lord Narayana in your mind and keep on repeating the mantra that I will teach you. This will make you concentrate on him.'

'But what does Lord Narayana look like?' asked Dhruva innocently.

Narada's eyes lit up. 'He is the most beautiful person you can ever hope to see, with large, dark eyes. He is tall and strong, with four arms. One hand holds a lotus; another, a warrior's mace; the third, a conch; and the fourth, a discus. His complexion is as dark and lovely as rainclouds. He wears a dhoti of brilliant yellow silk and a garland of wild forest flowers on his neck. He rides a great eagle called Garuda. There is no other like him.'

'What should I say to make him hear me?' asked Dhruva.

'It is the twelve-syllable mantra, the wish-fulfiller, "Om Namo Bhagavate Vasudevaya". Forget everything else and repeat it constantly, thinking only of him,' said Narada, and added kindly, 'If you ever feel afraid and want to go back, call out to me, and I will hurry here to take you home.'

'I won't,' said Dhruva, smiling happily, and did a pradakshina of Narada, that is to say, he went thrice around him and bowed in namaste. Narada gave him several more tips on how to meditate, patted his head and disappeared, again in the blink of an eye, leaving Dhruva to find his inner path to the Lord, if possible.

However, Narada resolved to also get help from the Seven Sages of antiquity who kept an eye on the world from their constellation of stars, the Sapta Rishi Mandala. The western world would come to call it Ursa Major.

~

After Narada vanished, Dhruva sat down as directed, shut his eyes and tried to conjure up a vision matching Narada's description of Lord Narayana. It took him some time to get the picture to his satisfaction, point by point. The last thing he attempted to visualize was Lord Narayana's face with big, dark eyes. At first, it was not easy to picture him without a visual reference to go by, but he thought again and again of Narada's description and finally succeeded. He went over each detail of the beautiful picture created in his mind's eye and softly began to chant the mantra 'Om Namo Bhagavate Vasudevaya', meaning 'I salute Lord Narayana', 'Vasudeva' being another of the Lord's names.

With this picture now fixed in his mind, Dhruva struggled to find a pattern to his breathing as advised by Narada. It took him three days, for the active little boy was unused to sitting still and developed terrible cramps in his arms and legs, while his neck grew painfully stiff. He felt hungry and thirsty, too, and got up from time to time to find berries to eat and water to drink. He fell asleep each night despite wanting to stay awake. Every so often, hot tears flooded his eyes when thoughts of his unloving father intruded. 'Why don't you love me, Father?' he wept in desolation and cried himself to sleep on many nights.

But Dhruva's little heart burnt with determination to find Lord Narayana, and if this was what it took, he was resolved to do it, no matter how difficult it was. A week went by and a month, and Dhruva got better and better at sitting still and meditating. In that first month, he lived off forest berries, but after some time, he decided to stop looking for berries and ate the grass that grew around him. This was not as hard to do as one may imagine because by that time, Dhruva had got used to austerity. The tearful bouts gradually stopped, for Dhruva's mind was now engaged more and more with his breathing. It was as though a deeper, stronger rhythm to existence had taken hold of him, and his hurt and anger gradually faded and fell from him like dried leaves from the twig.

By the third month, which he noted by the waxing and waning of the moon as also advised by Narada, Dhruva felt a strong disinclination to eat anything at all. Eating was a distraction from meditating, which had grown more and more intense for him. He decided that it was enough to live on water.

Dhruva's childish chubbiness fell away from him, his uncombed hair grew long and matted, and his clothes fell away in strips, leaving only his loincloth.

After the fourth month, Dhruva left drinking water. The vision he had in his mind of Lord Narayana grew more and more focused every day. He was completely entranced by it and grudged even a moment spent away from it. He now lived on air alone, and his little brown body looked like a wooden statue. His grief became subsumed in the intense feelings he had developed for the vision of Lord Narayana. From pining for his father's affection, his heart now ached for a loving response from the Lord himself.

Dhruva's tapas or austerity did not go unremarked. How could it, when the heat it generated in the atmosphere began to threaten the very cosmic balance? The Devas, or celestials in heaven, felt their golden world slide and shake, and they feared Dhruva.

Indra, the crafty king of the Devas, launched a series of attacks on Dhruva to break his meditation. There were no tigers in Vrindavan, but Indra produced one by magic and sent it roaring at Dhruva. But so lost was Dhruva in deep contemplation of Lord Narayana's vision that he did not even open his eyes.

Indra next sent a malignant serpent of enormous size to coil tightly around Dhruva's little body and devour him. But the Sapta Rishis or Seven Sages, who were warned by Narada to look out for Dhruva, struck down the serpent with their yogic power.

In a third, desperate, move, Indra called up a troop of evil spirits from the netherworld to harass Dhruva. They whooped and capered madly around the still little figure and emitted the most blood-curdling sounds, but so deep was the child's absorption in Lord Narayana that he did not even flicker an eyelid.

At this, the Devas panicked and went as a body to Lord Brahma, the Creator. 'Grandfather, do something! This has never happened before. All creation is finding it hard to breathe because of the heat produced by this child's meditation. Heaven itself is tilting. Please save us!'

Lord Brahma then spoke to Lord Narayana. 'Dhruva is so intent on seeing you that he has now become a threat to normal beings. Please take pity on him and on us.'

'I will. He has been fixed and immovable, like the meaning of his name "Dhruva". He is the most extraordinary human child I have ever seen,' said Lord Narayana.

He got up to go appear to Dhruva but suddenly checked himself. 'The child has a particular vision of me to which he has dedicated his being. If I don't appear as he imagines me, he will be disappointed.'

Saying so, the Lord summoned his great eagle Garuda and mounted his back, in full regalia with his four hands holding the conch, discus, mace and lotus, and the vanamala, the garland of wild forest flowers, flung fragrantly around his neck.

~

Dhruva sat lost in the vision of Lord Narayana that had grown steadily more luminous with every passing week. His breath had grown stiller and stiller and his body felt weightless. But suddenly the vision completely blacked out. Dhruva cried aloud and opened his eyes.

But what was this? There before him stood Lord Narayana himself in four-armed glory, with Garuda beside him. Dhruva stared speechlessly at the Lord's dazzling splendour. A kind smile hovered on the Lord's lips and his deep, dark eyes – even lovelier than Dhruva had imagined

– looked affectionately at him. Words tumbled over each other in Dhruva's throat, but he was unable to speak. The Lord understood his plight. He leaned forward and gently touched Dhruva's quivering cheek with his conch. At that, grateful, happy words leapt out of Dhruva's mouth, and he fell flat at the Lord's feet.

Raising him gently, the Lord said, 'Make your wish, Dhruva.'

But Dhruva shook his head with sudden, overwhelming clarity. 'Having seen you, Lord, I don't need anything else.'

'Your staunchness will not be in vain, my littlest devotee. Go home now. Sage Narada is already on his way to take you back. Your father will welcome you with love, and you will be king one day. When your time comes, your soul will come to me, and I will place you above all the world as a shining star in the sky, as fixed and steady as you have been in my devotion. You will be immortal.'

And so it was, and so it remains until this very day. 'Dhruva' is still our name for the Pole Star.

Dhruva, in Indian astronomy, is the North Star or Pole Star, above the constellation Ursa Major.

3

The Jujube Girl

What do you do when fate suddenly hands you the world on a golden platter and as suddenly takes it all away? Malati's story is about trying your best anyway. This story is found in the Sujata Jataka and, among other things, tells us that the ber was greatly relished in ancient India. The dramatic turnaround in this cautionary tale of 'The Jujube Girl' contains a teaching, as it is with all Jatakas. The word 'jujube' comes from the ancient Greek word for it, 'zizyphon'. It is also called 'Indian jujube' and 'red date' in English. Its Hindi name is 'ber'. Cultivated commonly in India, its small oval green fruit turns red and eventually wrinkles like a date.

'Fresh jujube juice! Just a pana for a cup!' called Malati at the market square of the busy Sravasti city, the capital of the great kingdom of Kosala. Malati was sixteen years old and the only daughter of a widowed mother. She lived near the woods, on the outskirts of Sravasti, where ber trees grew in plenty. She collected the fruit early in the morning, crushed them for juice in a heavy stone quern and strained the juice through cloth into a large earthen pot that she loaded on a pushcart along with a dipper and a number of little earthen cups. She made her way each day to the heart of town, where she attracted good custom as much for her looks as for the benefits of drinking ber juice.

The townsfolk found jujube juice a pleasant drink in the mid-morning heat, and its qualities were commonly known to all. This health-loaded fruit cooled the body, soothed sore throats, improved digestion and even served to calm nervous irritability. Some people drank it at night as a mild sedative, while knowing mothers quietly made their children drink it as soothing syrup when out travelling. Nobody objected either that the jujube juice seller was a very pretty young girl.

That morning, Malati was in particularly good form. She was freshly bathed and dressed in a new green sari that had been a gift from her visiting aunt, and she had tucked a string of jasmine in her glossy black hair. Her skin shone with the glow of youth and her big, brown eyes looked merrily at the passing crowd.

Suddenly, the noise of the town square was cut through by a loud drumbeat. It was the king. The praja, or subjects, dutifully stepped back in rows to allow the king's elephant passage. Malati stared wide-eyed at the procession, an arm akimbo. She looked as pretty and graceful as a statue of a dancing girl, but she did not know it. However, the king, atop his elephant, noticed. He took in the delightful sight of this shodashi, a sixteen-year-old piece of youthful perfection, and wanted more. Turning to his chief adviser, who sat with him in the royal howdah, he said in an urgent whisper, 'I must have that girl! Get her to the palace, will you?'

'My king, she is a poor seller of jujube juice. What will you do with a girl like that? Also, the praja will talk if you just help yourself to one of them. They may even protest, which will bring shame on the throne,' said the canny adviser who was none other than the Bodhisattva, the Buddha, in an earlier birth.

'I will marry her, of course! Why should anyone mind?' said the hot-headed king, who was twenty-three years old and fully convinced of his role as a devraj or 'god king' who ruled by 'divine right'.

The Bodhisattva knew that it was of no use to persuade the king otherwise when he was in this death grip of sudden attachment. Not only was he the king, with absolute power, and the lord of life in Kosala, but he was also young, headstrong and used to having his way. Since it was a personal matter and not one of policy, the Bodhisattva said no more but signalled to a guard on horseback to step up. 'Bring that jujube girl to me when I return to the palace,' he said in a low voice, and that was that.

Malati, to her utter amazement and delight, was married to the king with her mother's glad consent. He even made Malati his chief queen. She was allotted a splendid suite of rooms near the king and had ten maids to attend to her every need and wish. The royal cooks outdid themselves for her, hoping to overwhelm her digestion with rich food, for everyone was jealous of her sudden good fortune. But Malati proved to have a stomach of cast iron. She not only survived but thrived on a steady diet of roast venison, braised peacock, curried rabbit and pigeon pakoras, and also began to regularly order other such newly discovered delicacies as roast quail in butter sauce and puree of prize mangoes from the royal orchards with thick, sweetened cream scented with saffron.

The royal tailors fashioned marvellous confections of silk and gauze that made her look a thousand times more beautiful, while the king himself fastened new jewellery on her every other day – necklaces, earrings, bracelets, armbands, golden girdles, golden anklets, and rings for every finger.

The Bodhisattva gently suggested a tutor to teach her reading and writing, but Malati couldn't be bothered. She was too content as she was, sleeping late, waking to a leisurely morning meal, bathing, being dressed, strolling in the king's pleasure parks, eating sumptuous lunches and dinners and welcoming her husband at night in her strong, young arms.

The king was highly pleased with her and paid no attention to the Bodhisattva's practical advice that even if the chief queen was illiterate, she should at least learn to perform the religious rituals of the royal household. 'Oh, my other queens can do all that, this one is purely for my pleasure,' said the king airily, and once more, the Bodhisattva fell silent.

It was hard for him to dislike the king, though, for the king did not tolerate corruption and was keen to do the right thing by his people and country. He brooked no interference in his private life but was ready to learn in all matters of policy. He proved to be a highly accountable ruler who disliked flattery and valued honest, straightforward people of all ranks. He often went about in disguise through Sravasti with the Bodhisattva, observing his people and noting their views on various matters, and he was diplomacy personified, with not a shred of temper in his dealings with neighbouring kingdoms. The Bodhisattva grew to like him very much indeed, for despite his hot-headedness, the king tried sincerely to be a good ruler, which made him popular with his people.

The king set out one day for a long tour of Kosala and when he returned after several weeks, a welcome banquet was held at the palace by the Bodhisattva. Malati, as chief queen, was seated next to the king and did full justice to the feast. As the meal progressed, a golden dish heaped with jujubes was brought by a server. The king helped himself liberally, but Malati flushed in sudden embarrassment. Was this a slight from the royal kitchens? Were the servants making fun of her?

Trying to cover up, she asked the king in a high, artificial voice, 'Oh, and what are these things?'

The king stared at her in disbelief and lost his temper. 'Why are you putting on such airs?' he said, disgusted. 'I detest such vulgarity. Leave now. I am divorcing you; you are unfit to be queen.'

Malati left the banquet hall in tears, unable to look anyone in the eye. Back in her rooms, a maid packed a modest bag for her; all the jewellery and fine clothes were taken away, and a humble cart took her back to her mother's home. Her life as a beloved, pampered queen was over.

~

Malati shamefacedly kept indoors at her mother's house, for whenever she stepped out, she was the target of unkind laughter and gossip. The praja were clear in their feelings; their king was a good king, and Malati, merely an upstart who had proved unfit for her great position.

Malati's shame and humiliation were compounded by her mother's sarcasms, for the lady was a woman of principle and greatly disappointed in her daughter. She had refused to live in the royal compound and preferred an independent life in her old neighbourhood. But what broke Malati's heart the most was the loss of her husband. She loved the king deeply and cried herself to sleep every night thinking of him. To never see him again, to lose his respect and fall so low in his esteem, was the worst kind of suffering.

She stayed at home for the best part of the day, often breaking down in tears at the cruel blow fate had dealt her. When she stepped out to buy vegetables, every sneer, every whisper, every rude remark behind her back stung her like a red-hot arrow. Her grief and loss affected her appearance. The sparkle vanished from eyes that cried so much each day. Her youthful glow faded as her skin grew dull and lustreless from not eating right and staying indoors. Malati simply didn't know what to do next, and spent the day cooking and cleaning since that was all she knew how to do.

Making their simple, everyday food, Malati would suddenly remember the delicacies she had fed on at the palace and start to cry, not because such food was beyond her means now, but because it had been yet another expression of the king's love and pampering. She cried so hard one day that she almost sliced off her finger, chopping through a mist of tears. To sprinkle salt on her wounds, malicious neighbours would drop in from time to time out of curiosity and make arch remarks about another marriage, invariably saying, 'But who will touch the king's leavings?'

Such remarks cut Malati to the quick but more than anger, it was her grief at losing her beloved husband that tormented her. 'Why didn't I pay more attention? Why was I so foolish?' she berated herself night after long night.

Several months passed in a haze of misery. But charity came knocking in the strangest way one day, when a middle-aged man with a sensible face came by to their house. 'The king's adviser has sent me to you,' he told Malati. 'He is a man of great compassion and is troubled by your situation. You are living a quiet life and have not spoken ill of the king or got involved in quarrels with unkind people. I will teach you to read and write if you and your mother permit.'

'Of what use is an education to her now?' said the mother angrily, but Malati stepped forward. 'I don't know how it will help, but if it takes me closer to my lord's world, I am willing to try,' she said tremulously. And so began a marvellous year of learning. Malati not only learnt her letters but heard from her tutor, in much detail, about great queens in history and in the holy books who had behaved with impeccable dignity through the most horrifying circumstances. She was also taught about the personalities of great kings and how they chose to conduct themselves.

This exposure to a high standard of behaviour had its effect on Malati, who grew more thoughtful with every passing month. Since her mind was now stimulated, she also began to pay attention to her appearance again and gradually recovered her looks, although the old, carefree sparkle was long gone. What was the use of oiling her hair and washing it with soapnut powder if her husband was no longer with her to appreciate its silky gloss? Of what use was her glowing skin, burnished to a soft sheen with ubtan powder, when the love of her life despised her? Malati forced herself, however, to keep herself in good order, dress tidily and even wear a small string of flowers in her hair. Who knew what the future would bring? She did not want to be careless and let herself go even though she felt absolutely wretched and wracked by her loss.

A whole year went by with Malati doing her best somehow to keep up appearances and study, while steadfastly refusing to talk about her situation with anybody. It was the only way she knew of clinging to the shreds of her dignity and trying to face up to her loss. Gradually, her determination won her a level of outward peace although she still wept in grief at night for her beloved husband.

One day, Malati was favoured with a visit from the Bodhisattva himself, whom she received with great respect.

'You are only seventeen,' said the Bodhisattva, 'and you refused to learn the graces of your new life then. What do you feel like doing now?'

'I was ignorant and foolish. Everybody makes mistakes but mine was apparently too great. I should have understood my lord's character better and not pretended like I did. I will do anything to get my husband back,' said Malati forlornly.

'Are you brave enough to come to court and risk rejection?' asked the Bodhisattva.

'Yes, I am. At the very least, I will see him one more time,' said Malati.

'How will you approach him?' asked the Bodhisattva with an encouraging smile.

Malati thought hard and had a sudden idea. 'Shall I do this?' she asked the Bodhisattva, telling him her plan.

The Bodhisattva liked her idea very much and went away saying he would let her know a day in advance.

Back at the palace, the Bodhisattva found a suitable day in the weekly court calendar on a morning that petitioners from the praja were given audience with the king. After a few hearings, which the king responded to favourably, the court caller announced Malati and the king looked up with a frown. Modestly clad and looking lovelier than ever, Malati slowly advanced towards the throne bearing a jug of jujube juice. The entire court and all the assembled townsfolk gawked at her, but she paid no heed. Standing before the king, she bowed her head low and said softly and penitently, 'My lord, I was young and foolish. I am mortified by my behaviour. I love you with all my heart. Please won't you forgive me and take me back?'

There. She had staked her all in that one throw with those few honest words and stood trembling, unsure of her fate.

The king was still frowning, and the Bodhisattva decided that it was time to tell more truths.

'O king, her conduct has been irreproachable all this while. She has spent this whole year in getting an education to fit better into royal life. She has approached you with a jug of jujube juice to show you how sorry she is. King, it was your fault in the first place for elevating a poor girl to queen but not teaching her how to be one. Will you not forgive her now?'

The king's face cleared, and he looked at the Bodhisattva with affection and at Malati with new interest.

'What you say is true,' he told the Bodhisattva. 'I made her my wife without teaching her how to fit into her new life. It was indeed my fault in the first place, but she has more than met me halfway. I am happy to take her back.'

Saying so, the king stepped down and took Malati's hand with a smile. They lived happily ever after that. Malati never put on empty airs again and neither did the king's love for her ever falter.

4

Karmabai of Puri

Loss after loss after loss. What do you do when fate batters you so hard? There are different versions of the tale of Karmabai of Puri and this story derives partly from folklore and partly from the *Bhakta Vijaya* of Mahipati, a book of saints, authored in Marathi in the eighteenth century and translated into English in the twentieth century. Karmabai is said to have lived in the early seventeenth century. She was apparently a Jat lady from Nagaur district in present-day Rajasthan who grew up in Puri and died there. The annual Rath Yatra of Lord Jagannath at Puri stops for a while at her memorial as it rolls on its way. It commemorates the extraordinary event that is believed to have befallen her, which rocked Puri and became part of the mosaic of Indian belief.

Karmabai's parents had made a long pilgrimage east to the holy city of Puri by the sea from their inland village in Rajasthan. They were so delighted by Puri that they decided to settle there in the protective shade of Lord Jagannath's great temple. Karmabai had an enchanted childhood by the shore of the tossing, foam-crested Mahodadhi, or Bay of Bengal, and by and by her parents found a nice boy for her and married her off.

Life was a dream of bliss for Karmabai in her new home. Her husband loved her deeply, and her in-laws were kind to her. She became a daughter to them, not a daughter-in-law. Life flowed smoothly and pleasantly in the round of daily life, the visits to fairs, the joy of festivals and the daily darshan of Jagannath, Lord of the World, in his mysterious abode of great antiquity.

One day, Karmabai discovered she was pregnant. Delirious with joy, she eagerly anticipated the baby's arrival, sending special thanks to Lord Jagannath for this blessing.

When she was about three months along, her husband went on a journey to a nearby town on some work. He was supposed to return by dusk, but failed to appear. The little family was not unduly worried, thinking he would return by morning. But instead, a bullock cart trailed in at mid-morning bearing his corpse. Dhunu, for that was his name, had been gored by a rogue bull and had bled to death overnight. Karmabai's safe little world fell to ruins that instant.

'Dear Lord Jagannath, I wish to die, too. But I have to

live for my baby's sake,' she resolved, wiping away her tears. Her in-laws were numb with shock and could barely take two steps without collapsing in grief. The little house lay shrouded in a thick pall of gloom and Karmabai, out of concern for her baby, discovered that she was the only active person in the house.

After six months, Karmabai delivered a fine little baby boy. Her in-laws expectedly cheered up and named their grandson Raghu. A fresh wind of hope blew through their sad lives, and Karmabai vowed to make her child's life as full of warmth, love and care as she could.

Sixteen happy years went by in the joy of motherhood. The in-laws died along the way, but Karmabai got through it, somehow, thanks to the emotional security of having Raghu by her side. She was no longer a little girl but a woman who was used to dealing with difficulties and setbacks. Her parents had passed away and left her their property, which Karmabai rented to a neighbour's son. There was not too much money but there was enough to keep her small house in good repair, buy new clothes for Deepavali and feed Raghu well.

Besides learning to read and write at a small gurukul nearby, Raghu was set to learn a trade. He chose to be a carpenter. Taking inspiration from the wooden idols of Lord Jagannath and his siblings Balbhadra and Subhadra, he loved working with wood and soon turned highly in demand. He was devoted to his mother and no matter how busy he was, he always took care to run her errands and take her out on visits, encouraging her to spend time with friends and neighbours. A strong, pure happiness filled Karmabai's days again, different from her glorious days as a young bride but doubly precious, and she repeatedly thanked Lord Jagannath for it.

When she was convinced that Raghu was now a steady, responsible person, Karmabai cast about for a suitable bride for him. She found the ideal girl in Lakshmi, a trim, active person with a laughing face and a sunny, cheerful nature. After the small but perfect wedding, Lakshmi brought added cheer to the lives of Karmabai and Raghu. Just as she had been well treated by her in-laws, Karmabai made a daughter of Lakshmi and was well repaid with obliging and affectionate behaviour.

Raghu and Lakshmi were a devoted pair, and one day Lakshmi discovered that she was pregnant. Karmabai floated on her feet with joy at this glad news. She took to pampering Lakshmi with even greater care and love. But their happiness was doomed. One terrible afternoon, Raghu was brought in dead with his neck broken. He had fallen to his death from a high roof beam in a new house that he was building for a rich merchant.

Raghu's death shattered Karmabai's newly secure life all over again. Raghu was her darling, the focus of her life after losing her husband. How could she bear to go forward now? But who would look after Lakshmi and the expected grandchild if she failed them? Setting a stone in her heart, Karmabai turned resolutely to the task. Lakshmi, lost in grief, lacked no attention that a caring, loving mother could provide. Karmabai cooked her the choicest, most nourishing food and sang sweet songs in a bright, determined voice to infuse some cheer into Lakshmi's desolate face. It was a huge effort for her to put aside her own grief for Lakshmi's sake but she managed it somehow, weeping silently only when Lakshmi was asleep or out in the courtyard taking in air.

In due course, when a little grandson arrived, a fresh impulse of joy flooded the family. The baby brought tremendous happiness, as sound, perfect babies always do. The atmosphere of the house was miraculously transformed. Karmabai and Lakshmi chose the name Vishnu for the baby in honour of Lord Jagannath, it being one of his many names.

This new lease of life drove Karmabai into frantic, relentless activity. Her love for the lost Dhunu and Raghu lent even greater fervour to every motherly thing she did for Vishnu. She nurtured the baby with all she had, but Lakshmi proved to be another matter. Her cheerful, sunny nature could not withstand the tragic loss of her husband, and she went into a catastrophic decline, unable to eat well or sleep soundly and breaking into frequent, bitter bouts of weeping. Once again, it fell to Karmabai to be the pillar of the house. But her heroic efforts to pull Lakshmi along with her on the current of life proved unavailing. Eaten hollow with grief, Lakshmi slipped away into the night in the course of a severe monsoon chill. With a baby to bring up by herself again, Karmabai's back was against the wall.

'O Lord Jagannath, when will you stop testing me?' she cried in anguish before her chosen deity but received no answer that she could hear. Karmabai devoted herself to raising Vishnu tenderly as though he were a little godling. He was all that was left to her. He proved an absolute delight, clearly having inherited his dead mother's once-happy nature. Six happy years went by in this fashion, and, though haunted every day by thoughts of her lost ones, Karmabai fairly recovered her emotional buoyance.

One fine day, when the big annual fair called Bali Yatra was held on the beach to celebrate the voyages of ancient Indian seafarers across the Mahodadhi, Karmabai held Vishnu's hand tightly and took him to the fair. They had a wonderful time looking at the stalls and sampling the tempting fried bananas and sweet steamed rice in small bamboo holders. Wandering along the water's edge, Vishnu wanted to run ahead and Karmabai laughingly let him. Chatting with her neighbour, she followed placidly behind. This was Karmabai's stretch of coast, she had grown up by this shore as Vishnu was now growing up, and she smiled happily as the fresh sea breeze lifted the now greying curls on her forehead.

A sudden commotion made her look up in mild concern. The concern turned to alarm when she realized that the cause of the commotion was a little figure flailing out in the choppy waters and that it was Vishnu. As Vishnu struggled in the strong waves that had pulled him in when he ventured too far into the sea, several strong young boys plunged into the water to try and save him. But the waves had picked up force. The little figure went under and did not rise again.

This third, heavy blow completely stunned Karmabai. All purpose to her life was lost, and she did not know what to do with herself. Her valiant heart was finally shattered and she could not stop weeping. Her neighbour suggested she start taking in temporary lodgers from the pilgrim traffic that besieged the holy city of Puri around the year. Touched by the tragedy, the priests at Lord Jagannath's temple kindly offered to put in a recommendation to suitable travellers.

Lodgers began to arrive in ones and twos and for a small sum Karmabai provided them with food and a space to sleep for a few nights. Her staunch habit of active service made her attend to them with utmost care, but the spring was gone from her step and her face was unalterably downcast. Wild thoughts repeatedly surfaced in her head about walking into the sea in pursuit of Vishnu. When there were no lodgers to cook dinner for, she took to walking by the shore when darkness had fallen, and crying into the wind, 'Dhunu! Vishnu! Lakshmi! Raghu! Where are you, my darlings?'

It relieved her mental agony a little to walk by herself like this along the shore and keen into the wind. Surely, they could hear her, her precious ones? But the heartache came piercing back when she turned her lonely steps home. Karmabai began to invent household tasks that kept her up by lamplight, long after she should have fallen asleep. She endlessly rolled cotton into lamp wicks, polished every last brass bowl to a brilliant sheen with ash and tamarind, dusted and swept every corner and finally put herself to sleep on a reed mat, too exhausted to cry more. Each day seemed like a huge mountain to be climbed and activity provided the only way forward.

One week, a small band of saintly Vaishnava travellers arrived at Karmabai's house. Dressed in gerua, or ochre, they wore a calm, cheerful air and asked Karmabai's permission to sing a few religious songs before they retired for the night. Karmabai nodded listlessly and sat down to listen, her face falling into its now habitual look of misery.

After they had sung a few beautiful devotional songs, the leader looked compassionately at Karmabai.

'What troubles you, daughter?' he asked in a gentle voice.

Karmabai's composure shattered at his kind tone. She poured out her tragic tale, choking on sobs.

'Daughter, you are a brave, good woman. You have borne your great losses with courage. Now trust in God to show you the way forward. Will you do as I ask?' said the leader. Reaching into his cloth bag, he took out a small image of Vishnu as the baby butter-thief, Krishna.

'Treat this image as your child, feed and serve the Lord as devotedly as you did your family. Continue being kind to all. Then see how you feel about life after some time.'

Karmabai looked hopefully at the image. Could it really cure her misery? It was a well-made image of copper, and the expression on Baby Krishna's face was very sweet. She accepted it respectfully.

After this, it is safe to say that Karmabai went crazy.

Her need to love was so strong that it could not be satisfied with being kind just to the needy. She needed a person of her own to love; she needed to show her love in a thousand little practical acts of caring, for that had been her way her entire life.

Now she began to treat the little image as if it were a real, live baby. She lavished her love and care on it as tenderly as if she really were its mother. She bathed it in warm water, dressed it in scraps of the softest cloth she could find, and – refusing to feed a baby a rich, heavy diet of butter – she mashed soft rice in buttermilk and begged the baby to eat, eating the leftovers herself as mothers have since the world began. She began, insensibly, to feel better as the months passed. It was like having a doll or a pet and gave her something to do beyond cleaning the house and cooking. It gave a new impetus to the day to have something to think of beyond her daily needs. The 'something' soon grew to be a 'someone', for when deep feelings are invested in anything, they animate the heart and acquire a life or spirit of their own.

Now this is where the legend of Karmabai takes over. The story goes that the Lord grew used to being petted and pampered by Karmabai. This belief comes from the emotional logic that as we see God, so we receive God. We are free to see God in the form that works best for us and is closest to our heart. Draupadi saw Krishna as her best friend, and hence, she was given the name 'Krishnasakhi' or 'Krishna's Friend'. Karmabai saw Krishna as her own little baby, and that is how she took part in God's divine nature of being all things to people.

One morning, Karmabai was a little slow in her daily chores and was late with Baby Krishna's breakfast. The Lord, goes the story, began to feel 'hungry'. This was his lila or the games he plays with devotees. So he whispered in the ear of a priest at Jagannath's temple, 'Tell Karmabai to feed me, I'm hungry for buttermilk and rice.'

Being a staunch devotee, the priest took the message as the Lord's wish and command and proceeded to Karmabai's house, gathering an ever-ready crowd as he went.

'Karmabai! Why have you not fed the Lord yet?' he demanded to know as soon as he entered. Greatly surprised that he knew, Karmabai rushed to make the Lord's plate ready. Prostrating deeply before Krishna's image, she apologized for being late and begged him to eat. To the disbelief and joy of everyone there, the buttermilk and rice slowly vanished bit by bit from the plate. The Lord had eaten!

A great cheer broke out and crying 'Joi Jagannath!' or 'Victory to the Lord!', everyone fell at Karmabai's feet. She became a saint that very moment. The legend of Karmabai is enshrined ever since in the annals of the Jagannath temple. Even today, the annual Rath Yatra, the chariot procession of the Lord, stops at Karmabai's memorial in respect.

What of Karmabai, though? The miracle of the Lord's love, as made outwardly known, was a great thing. But it was the inner miracle of transformation, of overcoming devastating loss through the habit of love that Karmabai cherished. She spent her remaining years engaged in doing good deeds for the pilgrim community and died at a ripe old age with the glad thought, 'Love has given me peace, dear Lord, and for this blessing a hundred births spent in thanksgiving are not enough.'

5

Jana Jaswant's Ordeal

Nothing hurts us more than being betrayed by those we love and call our own. The story of Jana Jaswant the merchant, is a tale of how the power of emotional conviction overpowers the grief of colossal treachery. Jana Jaswant was neither a saint nor a sage but a regular person of simple, straightforward piety, whose origin and whereabouts are unknown. Yet, this story gained a hold in the devotional landscape of India and found a permanent place in the *Bhakta Vijaya*, the Book of Saints, compiled by Mahipati in the eighteenth century in what is now Maharashtra. The *Bhakta Vijaya* has been translated into several major Indian languages and is frequently cited in religious discourses, and so Jana Jaswant's story lives on in the Indian mind. This version is a modern retelling.

Jana Jaswant was a devotee of Lord Rama and seemed to have been greatly blessed by the Lord. He had a loving wife and five healthy sons. Moreover, he was a millionaire many times over, for he had greatly expanded the family cotton business into oilseeds and agri-produce with a wide, loyal clientele. Jana Jaswant was an honest businessman and meticulously professional in his transactions and deliveries, and this unusual quality was greatly appreciated by those he dealt with.

'How can you afford to be so honest?' teased a cousin once.

'What I can't afford is having to hide my face in shame from my Lord Rama,' said Jana Jaswant, smiling.

This single-minded devotion found expression in other ways as well, for Jana Jaswant greatly admired Lord Rama's character.

'Look how the common people of Ayodhya loved him for his simplicity and good behaviour to all, high or low. They roared in approval when Rama's father, King Dasarath, asked them how they felt about making Rama the crown prince. They said, "He doesn't wait to be greeted; he greets the man on the street first. When he's out riding, he stops and asks after our well-being. He has no false pride, and he is always giving away things to the needy."'

'And look how he refused to take back the throne when it was offered to him,' put in his wife.

'Exactly. He was above greed. And so forgiving! When Kaikeyi went with Bharata to the forest to find him, he warned Sita and hot-headed Lakshmana to treat her with the courtesy due to a mother. He spoke lovingly and respectfully to Kaikeyi despite the terrible wrong she did him. He was generosity personified.'

But in private, Jana Jaswant's eldest son held a different view. 'I think Rama threw away his good fortune and wasted fourteen years in the forest,' he snorted scornfully, and his four younger brothers, who looked up to him as a leader, snickered in accord.

Happily, Jana Jaswant was unaware of this, for his sons carefully concealed their opinion. Meanwhile, he tried to live up to the ideal of Lord Rama's generosity.

'My wealth is a blessing from the Lord. I must share it in thanksgiving,' he told his wife earnestly and gave it away in sackfuls to hospitals, orphanages and dharamshalas – rest houses for travellers and pilgrims found so plentifully in town and country. He played glad host to wandering sanyasis and holy men of every hue and fed the poor bountifully on every son's birthday and on his wedding anniversary. He especially loved feeding the poor on Ram Navami, Lord Rama's birthday in the month of Chaitra (March–April). Nobody was turned away from his hospitable door.

This uplifted and elated state of affairs continued for many years. Jana Jaswant's wealth came to no harm from his determined generosity. Rather, as his good name spread, more business came his way, and he grew richer than ever.

However, his sons had grown up and watched, disgruntled

and dismayed, as their father's philanthropy continued unchecked.

'We must stop him. That's our money that he's constantly wasting on beggars and sanyasis,' said the eldest son angrily.

'We need a plan though,' said his subordinate siblings, 'We dare not tell him to his face to stop.'

'We'll think of something soon,' swore the eldest and went off to a drinks party with his close friends, the sons of other rich men whose fathers were enviably tight-fisted with family wealth unlike his own father.

Gossip flew around merrily at the drinks party and soon turned to their king who had newly ascended the throne.

'What manner of a man is he?' asked Jana Jaswant's son curiously.

His friend, whose father was a minister, laughed.

'As bad as can be. He likes the good life, and the prime minister has already warned him twice that the royal treasury is the kingdom's money collected through our taxes and not his private fund to have fun with.'

'How did the king like that? After all, he's a king.'

'He didn't like it at all. He would like to kill the prime minister but doesn't dare do it.'

Back home, the eldest son cautiously asked his father about the new king. The answer delighted him.

'The new king is a low-minded person and won't be good for the kingdom,' said Jana Jaswant. 'We must pray that he improves.'

Now this was just the ammunition that Jana Jaswant's low-minded eldest son had been hoping for. He went off jubilantly to tell his brothers and formulate a wicked plan against their own father.

Soon after, Jana Jaswant's sons went as a body to seek a private audience with the king. Their meeting was arranged by the minister's son.

'O king, we have come to complain about our father. We are your loyal subjects, but our father calls you low-minded. He is the richest man in five kingdoms. Yet he wastes his money on needless gifts to undeserving people. We have come to you to demand our share, Majesty, and we implore you to seize the rest of his wealth for your own use, for you are the king and own the wealth of your subjects.'

The king, who was really as low-minded as described, liked the idea very much. 'But what shall we do with your disloyal father?' he said.

'He is not our father but our enemy,' said the eldest son heartlessly. 'You may drown him in the river for all we care, Majesty.'

The king laughed a nasty, pleased laugh.

'Very well, then!' he said, and issued precise orders.

Jana Jaswant was dragged out of his prayer room within the hour while his wife wept and his sons looked on without a word. Instead, they went with the king's men to the riverbank where the king waited to enjoy the spectacle.

The king's men stuffed Jana Jaswant into a sack that they weighted with stones, tied a cord around it and threw him with a big splash into the river. The last sight Jana Jaswant saw before the sack went over his head was his eldest son's wide grin of pleasure at his father's fate.

Tossed into the river, Jana Jaswant struggled to breathe, and concentrated all his thoughts on Lord Rama.

'O Lord, I love you and have faith in you. I seek refuge in you. If I die – when I die – please let my soul come to you and escape another birth.'

Then, a strange and wonderful thing happened. A large tortoise swam under the sack and steadied it. Jana Jaswant's hands and feet were not tied, for the king's men expected him to sink at once in the stone-filled sack. So he was able to force open the mouth of the sack and swim up to the surface.

'O king!' he called from the water to his shocked and surprised ruler. 'The Lord himself has saved me. Now, what will you do with me?'

Amazed by this apparent miracle, the king stared open-mouthed at Jana Jaswant flailing midstream. His hard heart cracked and filled with repentance. Pushing aside the royal guards, he jumped into the river himself to bring Jana Jaswant to the bank. He apologized most sincerely to Jana Jaswant and dropped him home in the royal carriage. The five sons slunk away and did not have the guts to go home to face their father.

Jana Jaswant's wife welcomed him back with tears of joy. Husband and wife went together to the prayer room and bowed low before the image of Lord Rama to thank him for Jana Jaswant's miraculous deliverance. But a great sadness lay heavy on them at the perfidy of their sons.

Jana Jaswant searched in his heart for forgiveness, but was unable to find it. He wrestled for weeks with his paternal instinct to forgive and with the well-meant urgings of family and friends. But a terrible line had been crossed and his self-respect, the right and duty of every human being, would not allow him to go back. When he tried to recall memories of his sons as sweet, lisping children, he saw instead their cruel grown-up faces at the riverbank, rejoicing in the horrible death they had plotted for him.

The pain in his heart was unbearable. His thoughts raced up and down in frantic disbelief, his own sons, his darlings, in whom his hopes were invested. 'Hopes of what?' he asked himself, finally. 'That they would be good to us in our old age, that we would have the pleasure of seeing grandchildren through them, and that someone of my own would light my funeral fire? Are those even worthwhile ambitions? How selfish they sound to me now. We come alone, live for a little time with others and must go alone. Who are they to me, really?'

These cold thoughts were like a sharp knife slicing away the illusion promoted by society, which he had cherished all these years, that people should love each other, especially within families.

Jana Jaswant addressed himself to his beloved deity, Rama. 'You yourself had to face a great family betrayal, Lord. And yet you made no complaint. Who am I in comparison?'

He reread the Ramayana, lingering on the chapters where Rama's family came to him at Chitrakoot to beg him to come back to Ayodhya. But his heart burned in agony about his sons' betrayal and, perplexingly, he also felt coldly indifferent to them. He could not understand this paradox. He thought it over and gradually realized that love belonged to the past, anger to the present and indifference to the future. He no longer wanted to engage with his sons, they had forcibly removed themselves from his affections and become evil strangers.

'O Lord, I am unable to live up to your high standards in this matter,' he prayed to Lord Rama. 'I can never trust my sons again. My heart burns with fury at their treachery but has also grown stone cold towards them. What should I do now when they are clamouring to get back into my good graces?'

It was Jana Jaswant's wife who came up with a solution.

'Give them each a share of your wealth and send them away. They tried to kill you, my husband. I can never forgive them, either,' she said resolutely.

Though the sons were shamed into repentance by the miracle and tried very hard to reconcile with their parents, they did not yield.

'Go your way in peace,' said Jana Jaswant. 'Trust once broken is not easily repaired. You wanted my wealth. Well, here are five large shares of it. You will never be in want if you use it well. I have kept a portion for your mother's use and mine, and we will live according to our wish and continue with our charity. Now you may take your leave.'

The five sons shuffled off shamefacedly, their pleas and protestations having fallen on deaf ears.

To his wife, Jana Jaswant said cheerfully, 'Well, wife. It's true, isn't it? "Ram naam saga, baki sab daga".' Only the Lord's name is truly ours. Other relationships are but an illusion.

'But they were our own sons, whom we raised with so much love,' his wife could not help mourning.

'We did what we had to do. It is our fault if we expected love and gratitude in return,' said Jana Jaswant firmly and his wife nodded soberly at this incontestable truth of the human condition.

Husband and wife put away their pain with a big effort and carried on being as charitable as ever, for that was their way of being. Their lives were further enriched by the affectionate friendship of an unexpected ally, their reformed king, who couldn't get enough of Jana Jaswant's company. He visited often, sent fruit from the royal orchards, delicacies from the royal kitchens, new clothes and sweets for Deepavali, invitations to dinner and carriage rides in fine weather, in fact, all the thoughtful attentions that could be expected from five sons rolled into one. He felt keenly aware that he had been lured into committing great cruelty and injustice on an upright citizen and was anxious to make up for it, growing very fond indeed of Jana Jaswant.

As for the five murderous sons, no one knows what became of them, but common report has it that they were so shocked and frightened by the results of their wickedness that they took to the straight and narrow thereafter, and if there was no good, there was no bad either heard about them ever again. Nobody even knows their names whereas Jana Jaswant is known to and respected by millions long after his time.

6

Ananda and Samilla

How do you deal with loss despite being an ascetic who has renounced worldly life? The unusual story of Ananda and Samilla is found in the Ananusochiya Jataka, or Jataka 328, in the Pali canon. The gist of this curiously modern story was apparently told by the Buddha himself at his regular retreat at the Jetavana grove (now the Sahet-Mahet historical park in Uttar Pradesh). It is said that the Buddha saw a grieving landowner of the region who was lamenting a personal loss in utmost despair. So he went to call on him and, being respectfully received, told him this story to make him stop grieving and open his mind to the Way. The story resembles, in one part, the tale of King Kusa, after whom Kusinagara is named. That is where the Buddha attained his parinirvana or release from mortal birth. Incidentally, King Kusa's story is illustrated in the Ajanta Caves, and we may also find tantalizing glimpses of how Ananda and Samilla might have looked at Ajanta.

Once, the Bodhisattva, or the Buddha, in a previous life was born as Ananda, the son of a rich priest in holy Benaras. He was raised very tenderly as the only child, and when he was fourteen, he was sent away for four years to the great university of Takshashila to the north-west, to get himself a first-class education. When he returned, bronzed and bright, his parents declared he should marry.

Ananda stoutly resisted this cosy plan, for he was of a fastidious, ascetic temperament and was wholly untempted by the pleasures of normal life. This unusual choice upset his parents deeply. They badgered him day and night to get married. Finally, to buy peace and having plenty of money, Ananda went to a goldsmith. He gave detailed instructions, and the result was a golden statue of 'the perfect woman', beautiful in every respect.

Ananda brought the statue home and told his parents with a droll look, 'Now find me a golden girl like this and I suppose I'll have to marry her.'

'How did you, an avowed ascetic, describe so much female beauty to the goldsmith?' asked his mother, more than a little annoyed by her son's delaying tactics.

'Detached observation, Mother,' said Ananda loftily and went away smiling.

Undeterred by the difficulties, Ananda's parents made a plan. A palanquin was brought for the golden image. Ananda's father put together a team of reliable attendants and security guards from his big household and appointed a trustworthy relative in charge of the expedition. A circuitous route was plotted around Benaras, ranging many kos, and the team was told to take the image from place to place and find a girl who resembled it. Excited and amused by this novel expedition, the team set off on its explorations in great spirits, determined to bring home the very bride for the young master.

But weeks and months went by, and only the brief message 'No luck yet' reached the anxious parents in Benaras from time to time. They cast aggrieved looks at their darling son who always had his nose buried in a palm-leaf manuscript or sat meditating for what seemed like unnaturally long spells. He broke off only for exercise, striding up and down the banks of the Ganga until sun down.

'Why is this happening to us?' wailed the mother.

'Why can't he be normal like other people's sons?' grumbled the father.

Ananda tried again to reason with them.

'Mother, Father, celibacy, too, is an honourable lifestyle choice. It has existed for a long time in our culture. Not everyone feels the need to couple up.'

'It's not a normal choice, son.'

'Maybe not in your eyes. But it is a human choice. Surely the right to say "No" is as valid as the right to say "Yes"?'

'We don't understand you, son,' said his parents sadly, wanting but unable to because of their strong social conditioning. 'What we know is that after being a student, a man must become a householder and after his grandchildren are born, a retiree ... and a renunciate only at the end.'

'You know I need your permission before I can ask a guru right now to give me diksha, or liberation, to be a renunciate. Call back that statue. Enough of this silly plan. I thought of it only to buy some peace. There is nobody like that.'

'You will never have our permission to take sanyas, son. Marry, you must.'

'You are unrelenting, Father, but I will find a way.'

Meanwhile, the statue of the perfect woman was taken to many cities and towns, and even villages, without a shred of success. Many hopeful candidates showed up as word spread in place after place, of the rich Benaras boy looking for a beautiful bride. But one after the other, they had to go back, for no one came close to the perfection of the golden statue.

At last, the team completed its by now weary march and turned back to Kashi, or, that is, Benaras. Halting for a day's rest at a small town not far from Kashi, they placed the statue in full view as usual, not expecting results. But a number of townsfolk stopped to stare at the image in surprise and finally asked the team, 'What are you doing with a statue of Samilla?'

The suddenly invigorated team made eager inquiry and hurried to the house of the priest whose daughter 'Samilla' was. Samilla or Samillabhashini turned out to be sixteen years old, beautiful beyond compare, but quiet and reserved. The team was delighted. However, Samilla had led a sheltered life and had strong views on peace and privacy. When her parents informed her of the proposal, far from being happy, Samilla refused to get married. 'I have no wish to be a housewife and a mother,' she said firmly. 'When you die, I will become an ascetic. Please don't force me into marriage.'

'Are you insane?' exclaimed her parents and sent her off with the team, escorted by a family team of their own. Received joyfully by Ananda's parents, Samilla looked even lovelier than the golden image, a flesh-and-blood beauty of the highest degree.

Ananda and Samilla were both married against their wishes. On their wedding night, Samilla, without a hint of shyness, coolly informed her brand-new husband, 'I am an ascetic by temperament and choice. I rejected the marriage bed before the wedding and reject it now. My parents forced me to marry against my will.'

Ananda's eyes lit up.

'You too?' he said with relief and happiness. 'You are the perfect bride for me then.'

Asking Samilla to sit comfortably, he told her his story and drew out hers. Talking late into the night, they agreed to live together peacefully without physical intimacy. They went to sleep at the two ends of the bed in inviolate peace and slept soundly.

After that, although Ananda's parents did not suspect a thing, Samilla and Ananda lived a life of perfect mutual accord. They went to sleep every night in the same bed but did not touch each other. To all outward appearances, they seemed a nice, normal couple, an impression helped by the fact that over the months they became very good friends, mutually respectful and interested in the other's thoughts and opinions. Samilla was always ready to hear about Ananda's studies and also took to efficiently managing the family's vast landholdings and its shops. She proved to have a great talent for it.

Ten pleasant years went by like this. If Ananda's parents wondered why no children blessed the marriage, they did not dare say so to the obviously devoted pair. And what a boon and a blessing Samilla proved to be in keeping accounts, seeing to staff matters and keeping the family holdings in top order.

'You do the work of ten sons!' they exclaimed fondly, presenting her rich, new silks for Deepavali, and forbore to ask, 'But why haven't you produced a child yet?' They had long banned their relatives from asking Samilla or Ananda such natural but intrusive questions.

In the tenth year of their marriage, Ananda lost his parents to an epidemic that suddenly swept Kashi. After performing their funeral rites, he had a serious talk with Samilla.

'Since my parents are now dead, I no longer have to pretend to be a householder. Your parents are dead, too. You have inherited many crores from them. I will give you everything that has come to me. Take it all and start a new life. Marry someone if you so wish. I want to take to the road as an ascetic with only a begging bowl. As you know, that has been my dream, right from my student days. I am finally in a position to follow my dream.'

'I don't wish to be a householder either,' said Samilla, as seriously as Ananda. 'I managed your family properties only because I felt it was my duty. I, too, will become an ascetic and wander with you. It is my dream, too.'

'Come, then,' Ananda smiled. They drew up a plan to distribute all their wealth to various charities and worthwhile causes. When this was done, to the amazement of their relatives who were unable to stop them, Ananda and Samilla set out happily in the simplest of clothes, each with a begging bowl.

They made their way across the upper Gangetic plain to the lower foothills of the Himalayas, where they lived on roots and fruit, rejoicing in the clean air and golden silence. A deep peace enveloped them, and they felt immensely grateful for their good luck in having a friend and partner who respected their choices.

After some years, however, they decided to return to the plains for salt so that their teeth would not fall out before time. They went back to Benaras and in that proud city, where they had once lived like kings and queens, they set off every day on separate paths to beg for food. They spent their nights sleeping in the outdoors in the beautiful royal parks of Benaras, in which lotuses bloomed in golden ponds, birds sang and graceful herds of spotted deer grazed and bounded.

One day, while in Benaras, Samilla ate some spoilt rice that she had been given in alms. Within an hour she was wracked by the most terrible dysentery. Ananda led her gently by the arm to rest in a shaded public hall and went out to beg for himself. When he returned with food, he found many people gathered around Samilla's still form, exclaiming and lamenting. Her delicate frame could not withstand the pain and she had died in agony while he was away.

Looking at his wife's lifeless form on the bench on which he had laid her, Ananda saw her as she was when alive. A hundred images of Samilla laughing, talking, sleeping curled up, meeting his laughing eyes with a laugh in her own, revelling in their secrets, flashed in his mind's eye.

But sitting with an emotionless face on the bench where she lay, he began to calmly eat the food in his bowl. The people around them could not help asking, 'Holy sir, who was this beautiful female ascetic?'

Ananda replied, 'When I was a householder, she was my wife.'

'Sir, why, then, do you not weep as we do? We are merely passers-by, yet we are unable to hold back our tears at this pitiful sight. And she was your wife! Explain it to us; we are greatly disturbed by this. Please do not leave us in the dark.'

Ananda rinsed his mouth and asked them to sit around him.

Thoughts that he had only ever discussed with Samilla poured out of him now in sudden inspiration.

'I choose not to grieve, which is why I do not weep. This

is how I see it. When she was my wife, you could say that she belonged to me in some way, and I belonged to her. But nothing is permanent. All of us have to go one day. She made her choices like I did and now she is gone, taking nothing with her. She had to go, if not today then another day. Or perhaps I would have gone first. But go we must. So why should I weep?'

'Sir, what you say rings true,' said a man. 'But what about love and friendship? How can we not mourn the passing of these? How can we not pine for those we have loved and lost?'

'Indeed, we cannot live in total detachment. But we need acceptance and detachment when someone's time is over, because we, too, will be gone one day. There is no escape from that so we may as well accept it.'

Saying so, Ananda swung up Samilla's lifeless body on his shoulder like how Shiva had carried Sati and began to make his way to Harishchandra Ghat to have her cremated. A number of people followed him in sympathy and when the funeral was done, they saw Ananda calmly pick up his begging bowl and leave Benaras forever.

He never came back to the plains but went to live alone in the Himalayan foothills where he and Samilla had spent so many years in perfect harmony. He thought of Samilla every day despite his philosophical talk. His heart ached despite what he had said to the people of Kashi. This was life, was it not? People came and went. There was nothing you could do about it except to accept it and try to live your turn out as harmoniously as possible. But the words he had heard in

Kashi haunted him: 'How can we not pine for those we have loved and lost?'

Ananda was forced to realize the truth of the human condition. It was all very well to uphold detachment at the intellectual level. But what could convince the heart? What could heal the grief of lost love?

Ananda realized too late that he loved Samilla and she had loved him, becoming his ardhangini or half his being in every other way but the physical. And yet, it was physical too, for had they not shared every meal, built every shelter and slept side by side for years? They had been life partners, with a unity of thought and purpose despite their celibacy. How lonely it felt without her. How was he going to deal with it? There was no one any more beside him to admire a view, to run laughing from the rain, to point out a flowering tree or creeper, to chat with cosily before drifting off to sleep, to walk the long miles with in companionable silence and little bursts of song.

He had no choice now but to reconcile theory with practice.

Ananda tried to reduce this unwanted pain in his heart by rebuilding an ascetic routine. He collected nuts and berries that he shared with the wild birds. He made friends with the wild creatures around him and was visited regularly by even the timid musk deer, while the Himalayan bears left him alone without showing either fear or anger.

He prayed and meditated every day, for he could not solve the puzzle that was existence. Why were people born, he asked himself. What was the point of love when it only led to parting and heartbreak? It was only a hedge against the darkness, deluding people for a while into thinking that all was well. But it inevitably fell apart. What, then, was the point of existence? The more he thought of these things, the more Ananda reviewed his own life choices. How callow and sure he had been. It was just incredible good luck that Samilla had come to him and given him a sense of life. He had felt human emotions like love and loss, thanks to her. 'Is that something worth having, after all?' he wondered, recalling Samilla's beauty, her good nature and her warm smile.

Ananda lived for twenty years like this in solitude and contemplation and was never completely sure that he had found answers that made complete sense or satisfied him. Every time he made a case for detachment and its consequent absence of pain, it would be countered by the human reality of the person that had been Samilla. Ananda slowly grew into the idea that to be attached was normal for a human being. It took great self-control and, above all, sadhana, or practice, to completely free oneself from earthly bonds. He resumed meditation with greater zest and began to find peace bit by bit. It was a delicate peace, like a fine piece of Benarasi muslin, shot through with the golden threads of Samilla's memory. He was happy that his mind grew stiller with every passing year, until he too died one day, painlessly, and one with his sylvan surroundings.

'I was Ananda in that birth,' said the Buddha to the grieving landowner who inconsolably mourned his dead wife, 'and Yashodara, my wife when I was a layman, was Samilla.'

7

Eknath the Orphan

A happy little boy suddenly loses his parents. Life stretches fearfully ahead. What is he going to do? Eknath (c.1533–99) was a saint-composer of the Marathi Bhakti canon. He was born and died in the historic town of Paithan in present-day Maharashtra. Paithan, or Pratishthana, is mentioned as far back as in Valmiki's Ramayana, and in the first-century Greek geography book *The Periplus of the Erythraean Sea*. It is well known today for its expensive silk saris, but few know that it was the seat of the Satavahana kings in the second century who ruled a very large part of India in their time.

Paithan was also an important place in the medieval Bhakti landscape, being associated with many great saints of the age, including Sant Jnaneshwar. Eknath's writings live on as a vibrant part of this heritage. Among other things, he composed a version of the Bhagavata Purana and the Ramayana, and a body of devotional verses. There is a big religious fair held every March, even today, at Paithan to commemorate Eknath.

Eknath was named after one of Lord Shiva's names. It was a heavy name for the little boy to carry, in meaning if not in length. But his mother, Rukmini, and father, Suryanarayan, never let him feel the weight of the name they had given him. Instead, his mother told him many stories about the life of Sri Krishna, especially about his divine childhood, which Eknath loved.

Suryanarayan was a kulkarni or tax accountant working for the government of their home town, Paithan. Located on the east bank of the great and beautiful river Godavari, the town was very nice to live in. Eknath loved Goda, as they called the river, and played happily on its bank with the other little boys in his lane. The family would go on picnics by the river on holidays, spread a cloth under a shady tree, and peacefully eat lunch as they watched the river flow past. Being near Goda made them feel light and happy, a feeling that little Eknath sensed as much as his parents did.

But one year, when Eknath was eight years old, Paithan was struck by cholera. House after house reported deaths, and funeral pyres burned all day long. The epidemic did not spare Eknath's happy little home. Both Suryanarayan and Rukmini died in agony, one after the other, and suddenly Eknath, the only child, was an orphan.

His neighbours led him gently through the funeral rites

that only he, little though he was, could perform, and Eknath went through it all in a daze, too shocked to even cry.

'Come and stay with us until we can decide what to do,' said his neighbour, and Eknath nodded mutely. He crept away to the riverbank where he had played and picnicked, making his way to the tree his parents usually chose. Sitting silently by the river, Eknath watched it flow with his mind blank. He began to say, 'Aai, Baba' from time to time, meaning 'Mother, Father' in his language, Marathi. Tears gathered behind his eyelids and slowly began to trickle out. Soon, they poured down his little face and, through it all, he kept saying 'Aai, Baba' in a broken voice until it began to grow dark and he had to get back.

Eknath slept deeply that night, the sleep of an exhausted child.

The morning brought a stern visitor, determined to do his duty. It was his grandfather, Chakrapani, who had unfortunately been away that week.

'You will live with me, of course,' he told Eknath, who shrank from him. 'Ajoba' as he called Chakrapani, meaning 'Grandfather', was very strict. He had left his boyhood far behind him and did not tolerate the pranks and games of childhood; the sudden need for a nap and the hunger for nice things to eat that only mothers made; the bedtime stories told in a sweet, steady voice that lulled little children so nicely to sleep; the hugs and kisses for no reason except the fond love of doting parents. Ajoba was a dour disciplinarian who led an austere life, immersed in his work as a deshpande or tax collector, and in the study of scriptures. There was no Aji or grandmother to soften the atmosphere, only a bad-tempered male cook who warned Eknath to keep out of the way if he didn't want to be branded with a piece of burning wood from the kitchen fire.

Poor little Eknath. His life changed completely. Chakrapani meant to do his duty, determined to bring up his grandson by the strictest of rules. He allowed only the plainest of food in his house, eaten for survival, not enjoyment. He had not tasted a fresh betel leaf in decades for he always kept it thriftily for the next day. He devised a timetable for Eknath that was more suited to an ascetic than to a bereaved eight-year-old boy.

Eknath had to wake up at four in the morning, bathe and drink a glass of buttermilk with some cold rice in it. After that he had to sit learning long Sanskrit prayers until five in the morning. Then came two long hours of grammar, followed by an hour of arithmetic.

They broke off then for the morning meal of rice, watery dal and occasionally a vegetable curry. Ajoba then left for work, giving Eknath homework for the day, which had to be produced in the evening for corrections and scoldings. More than one mistake earned a stinging rap on his palm from Ajoba's sharp cane.

Ajoba did not believe in affectionate words or praise. Such softness, according to his code, weakened the moral fibre. So he always spoke sternly and even harshly to Eknath.

Eknath was overwhelmed by this changed atmosphere.

His parents had spoken to him with love. Not a scrap of affection fell his way now. Eknath silently cried himself to sleep at night, missing his parents. He tried to console himself by remembering the tales of Sri Krishna that his mother had told him and whispering his mother's daily prayer to Ekvira Devi, their family goddess. He stayed far away from the bad-tempered cook and his burning brands.

The only time Ajoba softened was when he spoke of Bhanudas, Eknath's great-grandfather. Bhanudas had been a great saintly figure. He had gone south to the kingdom of Vijayanagar and, with much persuasion, brought back the sacred idol of Vithoba to Pandharpur, its original home by the river Chandrabhaga.

'Why is Vithoba so special?' Eknath had ventured to ask.

'He is Sri Krishna. He came to Pandharpur long ago to bless his devotee Pundalik and left his statue there, standing on a brick. It is a very holy place for us. Pilgrims called Varkaris go there every year in dancing, singing bands.'

'May we go too?' asked Eknath enthusiastically.

'You are going to Devagiri to learn the Vedas from a proper teacher. Don't disgrace me when you go there,' said Ajoba shortly and got up to leave without further explanation.

Eknath was afraid of this unknown prospect, but since nobody explained anything, he fell back on his personal prayers to give him courage. He was sent many miles away by bullock cart to the fortress city of Devagiri that had been renamed Daulatabad by its new Muslim owners.

Janardan Swami, his appointed guru, lived in Devagiri and held court every evening under a banyan tree, giving religious discourses. His followers came from all castes and communities. There were even a few Muslims, friends of Janardan Swami, who were attracted by his broad-mindedness and powerful storytelling.

Eknath felt lonely in the gathering. No one took notice of the solitary boy, and he felt awkward and unwelcome. He thought wistfully of his short life with his parents. Would no one ever love him again? 'Why did you leave me, Aai, Baba?' he asked pitifully every morning and every night.

Janardan Swami began to instruct him in the Rig Veda early in the morning, and Eknath struggled to learn the complex old metres and hard-edged words. But Janardan Swami had a busy job and could not instruct Eknath all day. He was the kiladar or governor of Devagiri fort, appointed by the Sultan, and had a thousand duties to attend to. He had accepted Eknath as a pupil only out of respect for his great-grandfather, Bhanudas.

As one day followed the other, Eknath struggled hard to find his place. He spent his morning in study, his afternoon in play with two other little boys who lived near Janardan Swami's house on the hillside, and his evenings listening to his guru's stories at the daily gatherings. His days took on a rhythm, but he constantly pined inside for his parents, for his lost family life and the Godavari. His playmates went home to their mothers, but Eknath had evening duties to attend to – fetching and carrying for Janardan Swami's brisk, busy wife, before he went to the courtyard to listen to his teacher's stories, always seated at the edge of the gathering.

One day, a band of Varkari pilgrims called on Janardan Swami. They sang and danced at the evening gathering about the beauty of Vithoba and his kindness to his devotees. Eknath's hungry heart lapped it all up, and he fell to thinking again about Sri Krishna but more deeply than he ever had.

'Here am I, without anyone to call my own and nobody to love me. And there is Krishna, whom everybody loved even when he was naughty. They say he is everyone's friend. That means he is mine, too,' he thought.

This realization changed young Eknath's life a great deal. From feeling completely lonely and neglected, he began to feel he had a secret friend in Krishna. He awoke thinking of Krishna, silently greeting him in his heart. He sat down to study with full interest, thinking of how Krishna had studied diligently at Rishi Sandipani's ashram at Ujjain.

He exercised daily, thinking of Krishna and Balaram wrestling for sport on the banks of the Yamuna. 'Ah, Goda, I was a little boy when I left your banks. But I'm growing up now and will see you again one day,' he promised himself. He grew very gentle with his playmates, thinking of how Krishna had protected timid Sudama at school, and they liked him for it and began inviting him home to eat the food their mothers had cooked.

He went to sleep at night thinking of Krishna's courage as he faced and destroyed one demon after the other, even though he was only a little boy. He ate cold rice and buttermilk with new relish, for was this not the very lunch that Mother Yashoda regularly packed for Krishna when he went to graze the cows with the other gopa boys in Vrindavan? Had not Veda Vyasa said so in the Bhagavata Purana?

His concentration and studies improved with this new cheerfulness and Janardan Swami took note. He began to take fresh interest in Eknath and instructed him on many important matters, literary and spiritual.

Several years passed fruitfully like this, although Eknath thought every day of his parents and his lost childhood home. Becoming aware of Krishna as his secret friend had helped him take on one day after the next, but his lonely heart could not be filled. He could never forget his parents and longed to return to Paithan. It was his lost paradise on earth, and all the Sanskrit verses in the world could not compare with the deep feelings contained in the words 'Father' and 'Mother'.

One day, Janardan Swami delighted Eknath by directing him to go on a pilgrimage: 'Your studies with me are now complete. Go to Lord Shiva at Trimbakeshwar and offer him your respects. After that you are free to go where you please. You may come back to me any time.'

Eknath took leave gratefully and left Devagiri forever.

'To Lord Shiva, first,' he thought joyfully as he strode along the highway. 'Then to Pandharpur to see Vithoba. But after that I will go back to Paithan forever to be near Aai and Baba's memories.'

8

Ranjit Raya's Daughter

How can a parent cope with the loss of a dearly beloved only child? The crux of this story is a parable told by Sri Ramakrishna Paramahamsa (1836–86) in the nineteenth century. It tells of a father and daughter who lived once upon a time near the village of Kamarpukur in what is now Hooghly district in West Bengal. Kamarpukur is the birthplace of Sri Ramakrishna. There is a branch of the Ramakrishna Mission there and a lake that was once called Ranjit Raya Lake. People hold an annual festival there in the month of Chaitra (March–April) in honour of his daughter, whom they considered of divine origin because of the supernatural tale attached to her. Sri Ramakrishna reportedly said when he had finished narrating this originally brief parable, 'Even Narendra (Swami Vivekananda) believes in these things now.'

Ranjit Raya was the landlord of Kamarpukur village. His family was an old, established one and his reputation was good as a fair and just man who was kind to the poor and hospitable to travellers. He was the owner of vast, fertile acres and had business interests in Calcutta as well. His time was gainfully spent in attending to his various duties and responsibilities. He was helped in life by his sweet-natured but strong wife, who took good care of his household and his relatives and servants.

If Ranjit Raya had one sorrow, it was that he had no children. He was a devout man, and in that 'Devibhumi', or Land of the Goddess that is Bengal, he began to pray, meditate and perform charities in the name of the Mother Goddess, Durga. This went on for several years, and finally he was blessed with a beautiful baby daughter. Her face shone with celestial lustre; her dark curls were most unusual for a newborn. And her eyes! Nobody had seen such large, bright, long-lashed eyes in a baby.

Ranjit Raya and his wife, Mrinmoyee, were convinced that the Goddess herself had manifested as their daughter because of Ranjit Raya's austerities. In gratitude, they chose the simple but powerful name of 'Devi' for their child.

Ranjit Raya adored his daughter whom he considered as prasad, or a gift, from the Goddess. The little one, too, was greatly attached to her father. She would not sleep at night unless her father put her on his shoulder and walked up and down, crooning to her. When she could walk, she took to following him around like a little shadow. He had to leave the house secretly every day to avoid making her cry.

Six years went by in this fashion, and Devi grew prettier and more endearing with each year. Besides her doting parents, the relatives and servants of Ranjit Raya's household loved her and spoiled her unashamedly for who could resist such a charming child. Secure in this unalloyed love, Devi grew quite bold and independent and ventured out into the garden to play by herself. But at the given hour she would run to the gate to watch for her father's horse carriage. The minute she spotted it, she would run towards it, and it became the practice that the carriage would stop and Devi would clamber into her father's arms to finish the drive to the house.

One day, Ranjit Raya sat in his office room in the house casting his annual accounts with his munshi or head clerk. Not just his estate, his business had expanded, and he had many matters to look over before paying his taxes.

Devi ran into the room before anybody could stop her to be near him. Seeing him preoccupied, she began to explore the room. Soon, with childlike excitement, she picked up first a glass paperweight, then the inkwell, then the blotter, a book, a desk clock, one thing after the other, and kept interrupting Ranjit Raya to ask, 'Father, what is this? What is this?'

Ranjit Raya tried at first to tell her nicely to stop disturbing him, but Devi persisted with her interruptions. Finally, the father said in a distracted tone, 'Just go away.'

Devi was so shocked by this that she ran furiously out of the house and out of the gates.

She overtook a peddler of shankh, or conch-shell objects, who was going by. She stopped him and asked for a couple of conch bangles for her tiny wrists.

'What about my money? That will be two coppers,' said the peddler.

'See my house there? There are two coppers in the little wooden box near my bed. Ask them at home for the money,' said Devi, sliding the bangles on her wrists.

Such was her charm that the peddler just nodded and went towards the house, not even bothering to ask where such a little girl was going on her own.

Devi went on her way, unnoticed, while the peddler made his way to the big house. There was an uproar when he asked for his money and they could not find Devi. The entire household ran about to look for her. They found the two copper coins exactly where she had said, but of the little girl there was absolutely no sign.

All at once, there was a commotion at the gate. A band of villagers burst in and told a weeping Ranjit Raya the terrible news. Devi had fallen into the lake and drowned. A little arm with conch bracelets on it had flashed above the water and gone under. It had all happened so fast that nobody could save her.

Ranjit Raya and his wife were devastated. But whereas grieving Mrinmoyee could distract herself with running the big household, nothing could make Ranjit Raya feel better. His estate agent tried to busy him with accounts and development schemes, but such well-meant efforts bounced off like dried gourds from the stone wall of Ranjit Raya's indifference.

He wandered around his house, garden and estate like a lost soul, barely ate and did not sleep well at night. Wherever his reddened eyes fell, he saw his little princess, laughing, playing, lisping questions.

'Why was I not more patient? Why did I tell her to go?' he lashed himself bitterly, for not paying just a little more attention.

But the copper sky blazed down deaf and the lake waters lapped and laughed, unmoved. The leaves on the trees seemed to rustle 'Too late, too late' at his anguish.

Months passed and Ranjit Raya felt no better. A dullness overcame his mind, and he could neither eat, drink nor sleep with comfort. Grief coloured the world grey and it angered him to see other people walking cheerfully by with their children beside them. Why was life so unfair? What had he done to deserve this when all his life he had been dutiful and affectionate, as a son, brother, husband, father and landlord? He had fulfilled every role to the best of his ability and was never behind in charitable works. Why, then, when he had lived life exactly as prescribed by scripture, culture and humanity, was he punished so severely by the death of his only child, the fruit of his penance and prayer?

The universe seemed cruelly random to him, without plan or purpose, without justice or mercy. Brooding on his loss, Ranjit Raya spent two whole years in grief and inactivity. He attended only absently to his business duties and came perilously near to losing some of his wealth had Providence not blessed him with a loyal and sincere estate manager, who steered him clear of trouble with respectful, gentle insistence.

Indifference led to ill health and aches and pains that Ranjit Raya ignored until his wife noticed and treated him at first with home remedies and then threatened to send for the English doctor from Calcutta.

Finally, Mrinmoyee approached him hesitantly, her eyes glistening with tears.

'She is the one who came to us as our child. Ask the Goddess why this happened,' she said.

Ranjit Raya gave a mighty start at that. Lost in grief, he had forgotten about the one he considered the cause of things. It was yet another reproach to rowel himself with.

He decided to take small steps to remedy this at least. The next morning, after his bath, he went to sit in his prayer room. He began by chanting the Goddess's name a thousand times to calm and steady his nerves. When he felt more stable, he began to speak to the Goddess in his mind.

'What did I do wrong, Mother? Why did you go? Why was my child suddenly taken from me? Why was I blessed with her only to lose her at such a little age, before she had a chance to live and grow?'

There was no answer, but Ranjit Raya felt a little lighter in his mind, having emptied his heart out to the Goddess. Surely she would answer him?

He soon grew obsessed with this daily one-sided conversation. Sitting in his cool, clean prayer room and talking to the Goddess became the high point of his morning, after which he found he was able to attend better to his estate duties. Months passed like this, and though the dull greyness did not abate, Ranjit Raya felt neither better nor worse.

One night, when absolutely not expecting miracles or visions, Ranjit Raya had a dream. The Goddess appeared to him in full splendour and spoke lovingly to him as he prostrated himself at her feet.

'Son, why are you upset with me? I am Mahamaya, the great illusionist. I create attachment, and you can only be free of me when you learn detachment. But not cold detachment. Oh no, never that! Devi finished her karma on earth and left. It is as simple and final as that. She was a pure soul and is back with me now. She is me. But look around you, son. You are responsible for so many people, for so many little Devis. They need your help.'

'How can I help them, Mother?' asked Ranjit Raya through his tears.

'Son, how do you see me?'

'As Sarasvati, Lakshmi and Durga, Mother,' said Ranjit Raya.

'What does that mean in real terms?'

Ranjit Raya thought for a minute. 'As knowledge, health, wealth and strength, Mother,' he said.

'Then you know what to do, son,' said the Goddess with a tender smile, and vanished.

Ranjit Raya woke up with a sense of excitement. He paced up and down, making plans all night.

After his morning tea, Ranjit Raya sent for his estate manager.

'Make a list of how many girl children there are in our village. Find and show me a good place in which to build a school. Ask the lady doctor who comes to our home to come on an inspection visit for two or three days.'

Having issued these startling instructions, Ranjit Raya mounted his horse and began to go from house to house on his estate. Instead of summoning the villagers all together, he went personally to each family to persuade them to let their daughters study at least reading, writing and arithmetic, for a couple of years each.

'I would have taught my daughter these things. Now please let me arrange to teach yours,' he entreated in each house. Taken aback and touched, the village agreed to this bold new experiment.

The school was built in two months, a simple mud and wood structure, and Mrinmoyee herself taught the girls for two hours, five days a week. Dr Samuel, the lady doctor from Calcutta, made regular visits to the school and advised the girls on health and hygiene, and how to look after themselves better.

After a few months, Ranjit Raya had another brainwave.

'It is hard to study on an empty stomach,' he told Mrinmoyee. 'I should have thought of this at first. I'm going to arrange for a midday meal. Khichuri one day, fruit and milk another day, vegetables and rice on another. Leave it to me, I will plan it.'

And so, the thirty-odd girl students also received food, which added to their value at home, for they became one less mouth to feed.

In this manner, Ranjit Raya tried to give the poor girls of his village some of the benefits he would have given his daughter. The villagers completely understood why he was doing it and indulged him. They did not let conservative elders or shocked relatives from the villages nearby object to daughters going out of the house.

'It's only in our own village, and the Raya's wife herself is the teacher. No harm can come of it,' they soothed agitated protesters.

A year went by, and two, and three, and the school flourished. The local British magistrate even came by on a visit and praised the pupils. Ranjit Raya was glad about it. His heart never healed completely, although over time, it began to hurt less, and he gradually made his peace with the lake and with the house and garden. But even ten years later, when his carriage entered the gates, his eyes would suddenly mist thinking of the little figure that would come running to be picked up.

However, the villagers gave him an unexpected gift.

'Your daughter was none other than the Goddess born to you. You have helped our daughters in her name. We will hold a fair each year by the lake to remember Devi on the day she vanished,' they declared.

And so, a tradition was born at Kamarpukur that comforted Ranjit Raya and his wife somewhat that their daughter would not be forgotten but had instead attained a long life in the hearts and minds of people.

9

Ravana's Mother

A mother loses her sons to the enemy but actually admires the enemy. How does she reconcile her grief with her sense of right and wrong? The story of Ravana's mother, Kaikasi, is mentioned in the Valmiki Ramayana in the Yuddha Kandam and in the later addition known as the Uttara Kandam. Kaikasi is called Nikasha in the Bengali Ramayana of Krittibas Ojha (1381–1461). Sri Ramakrishna narrated a brief parable about Nikasha in the nineteenth century. Her name hardly comes up in discourse, but this retelling attempts to talk more about her.

When they brought Ravana's body home to the palace from the battlefield, a great wail went up in the women's quarters. All his six sons had been killed in battle, one after the other, and so had his brother Kumbhakarna, the giant. And now their king, their hero, was dead. Ravana's wives led the lament. Mandodari, the chief queen, who had begged Ravana to return Sita to Rama, wept inconsolably.

Dhanyamalini, the younger wife, wept, too. She was a gentle, thoughtful person who was, however, too scared to voice her opinion and had never opposed her mighty lord Ravana, unlike Mandodari, braver and more outspoken, had. Dhanyamalini's four sons had fallen in battle to Angad the valorous vanara, nephew of Hanuman, who had set Lanka on fire just a few months earlier.

The women thronged around Ravana's bier, stroking his once mighty arms and wailing in sorrow.

In the commotion, nobody noticed what Nikasha, the old queen, did. She slipped out of the room and out of the now unguarded palace, taking only a change of clothes with her in a small bundle, and began to make her way to the hills outside the city.

'Halt!'

A troop of vanara soldiers suddenly blocked Nikasha's path.

'Who are you and where are you running away? Come with us to Rama!' they said and marched Nikasha off to the battlefield where Rama and Lakshmana sat with Ravana's brother, Vibhishana.

'Mother! What are you doing here?' exclaimed Vibhishana and went forward to bring her to Rama.

Lakshmana looked at Nikasha in surprise. Dropping his

voice, he said to Rama, 'Look at this old woman. She has lost her sons and grandsons, but she's running away because she wants to live longer even now!'

'Lakshmana, be respectful. Let us hear what she has to say,' said Rama.

Rama and Lakshmana stood up to receive Nikasha and Rama invited her to be seated. He looked at Nikasha silently. She was of medium height and slenderly built. Her silky white hair was elegantly arranged and her clothes were in muted good taste. She had beautiful cheekbones and delicate hands and feet.

So this was Ravana's mother. Rama could not relate this proud, slim woman to bull-like Ravana and the outsized Kumbhakarna. And then, he looked at Nikasha's eyes. They burned black with an inner fire.

'Queen Mother, I apologize for my soldiers. Please do not be afraid. You are perfectly safe and so are your daughters-in-law and palace women. I entrust you to Vibhishana's care. He will be king of Lanka now, and you must bless him at his coronation, which is tomorrow,' said Rama gently.

Nikasha looked back at him and inclined her head regally.

'Queen Mother, what made you leave the palace and set off on your own?' asked Rama.

Nikasha's eyes suddenly blazed, but she answered carefully.

'Rama, I thank you for your care. But you will not believe why I ran away,' she said in a sweet, low voice, the voice of the seductress who had trapped the noble Rishi Vishravas into marriage as a young woman, directed by her exiled demon king father, Sumali, and her shrewd mother, Ketumati.

'Tell me, Mother.'

Nikasha hesitated at first but found her voice.

'Rama, if I had wished, I too could have drowned in sorrow at the death of my sons and grandsons. I was furious that Lakshmana disfigured my daughter, Shurpanakha. But when I heard the full story, the right and wrong of it became clear to me. If she had not charged at Sita to kill her, Lakshmana would not have drawn his sword on her. He spared her life. Later, I pleaded with Ravana, as did Vibhishana, to return Sita to you and save Lanka from calamity. But he would not listen. Vibhishana, being a man, could leave the palace, fly over the sea and come to you. It was I who advised him to seek refuge in you after Ravana humiliated him for urging Sita's return. But how could I go, Rama?'

'I understand, Mother. But why did you leave now by yourself instead of staying behind with the womenfolk?'

'Rama, I did not leave in fear of you. I don't know if you will understand why I left.'

'I want to know, too, Mother,' said Vibhishana, while Lakshmana looked on incredulously. After Kaikeyi, he did not trust senior queens, especially the mother of Ravana.

'Rama, Rama, I don't know how to say this. I have heard of your every exploit from behind the palace walls. Our spies brought in detailed reports. I marvel at you, Rama. You left home without protest at your father's command, giving up the kingdom that was yours by right. You slew Khara and

Dushana and their entire army single-handedly. You set out to conquer mighty Lanka with no more than a band of vanaras. You compelled the sea god to bear your bridge to Lanka for a hundred kos. Our spies reported you command the hearts of your soldiers without ever raising your voice. Your wife stayed loyal to you despite every threat and every temptation. Who are you, Rama? There has never been another like you.'

'So why did you run away, Mother?'

'Rama, I wanted to live longer to see what else you would do.' And Nikasha folded her hands and looked steadily at Rama, hoping he would understand.

Lakshmana could not help a snort of disbelief, but Rama flung up his hand to stop him.

'Mother, we will stay in touch. Please return to the palace now and live peacefully in Vibhishana's care. He will not let you pine away.'

Nikasha was led away courteously by the guards and returned to the wailing women. She shut herself away in her chamber to think.

'My life has been tossed and turned by ambitious men and now I have lost them all except Vibhishana, the only one with a conscience,' she thought, with sorrowful insight. 'My father forced me to seduce and marry Vishravas to beget noble sons who would restore the fortunes of the demon race. My father did not love me at all; he only saw me as a political tool. My heart aches that my good, kind husband left me, sick of my ambition to make Ravana the king of Lanka. I spoilt him too much, my darling eldest son. Ravana broke my heart, snatching Sita away. How could he do that? I was so disappointed in him. I am bitterly ashamed of my life and its consequences. Rama is the first man that I fully respect. How can I atone for my mistakes and win his respect?'

Nothing, she realized, would change her unhappy life unless she took positive steps. She had power as the Queen Mother still, if Vibhishana was to be king. She would wait until after the coronation to put her plans to work.

After the conquering army left Lanka, the palace returned to peace and quiet. Keeping Rama's words in mind, Vibhishana entrusted the palace women's quarters to Nikasha's care, which had been Mandodari's responsibility for years.

Nikasha mourned her dead sons and grandsons deeply. Right or wrong, they had been the flesh of her flesh, blood of her blood. A thousand memories haunted her, especially of Ravana. He had been an affectionate son who had honoured her deeply and listened to her every stratagem. Except for two things. The first, when he had foolishly tried to uproot holy Kailash to bring Lord Shiva home to Lanka. The Lord had taught him a severe lesson, and only by composing and singing sincerely in Shiva's praise had Ravana's repentance been accepted.

His second error, of course, was kidnapping Sita. Ravana had discounted Rama as a homeless wanderer. Nikasha and Vibhishana had both pointed out to Ravana that to kill Khara, Dushana and the formidable rakshasa army single-handedly was not the work of an ordinary man. Nikasha wept inconsolably to think of the consequences of Ravana's adamant refusal to listen. She almost hated herself for admiring Rama. But her innate honesty could not be denied. Rama was the better person. Nikasha's grief was made worse by shame that she had failed to bring up Ravana better.

'How proud must you be, Kausalya,' she addressed Rama's mother in her mind. 'Your son is admired by all, even by me, while mine will be reviled forever.'

Despite feeling crushed by her leaden sense of grief, Nikasha made a sincere attempt to pull herself together. She no longer spent her days in idle luxury as she had when Ravana was king. She began to hold a morning meeting every day with her daughters-in-law, giving Vibhishana's wife, Sarama, due importance. During the meetings, she discussed the running of the palace and gave each daughter-in-law a charitable project to undertake for the welfare of Lanka's battered subjects. Many men were dead in battle, and Nikasha held a special widows' court every week to rehabilitate the partner-less women. Husbands were found for many from among the remaining men, and orphaned children were put up for adoption in suitable homes.

Nikasha inducted a number of poor, orphaned girls as palace maids and trained them herself in palace etiquette. She found them husbands among the soldiers and shopkeepers of Lanka. She made field trips to the countryside and asked the farmers about their problems, bringing the news back to Vibhishana for appropriate action.

She reserved afternoons for her remaining grandchildren, the girls, and the grandsons who had been too young to fight, and told them stirring stories praising Rama, not Ravana.

Unknown to anyone, she dedicated everything she did to Rama. This gave her charitable work an inner focus and a sense of reparation for the havoc wreaked by Ravana on his people. Constant activity gradually diverted her mind and wore away the sharp edge of her sense of loss. When she broke down, she did so in the privacy of her chamber, refusing to cry before others, even her daughters-in-law. She did not care if people gossiped about her unblinking outward composure. Her feelings were her own and not for public display.

A chastened Shurpanakha took her cue from her mother and lived quietly in the palace until the day she drowned in a boating expedition. Nikasha mourned her passing with ever-increasing quietness, unlike her daughters-in-law, who had cordially disliked their spoilt sister-in-law and her haughty temper when Ravana was king.

The years rolled by and Nikasha lived for the times when messengers would come to Lanka bearing greetings, news and gifts from faraway Ayodhya. Rama kept his word and wrote a letter just for her, inquiring about her well-being. Nikasha stored the letters in a carved sandalwood box that she kept in her prayer room next to the Shivlinga and offered flowers and rose water to the box with her daily prayers.

She never let the messengers return without carrying

her personal gifts for Rama and Sita in addition to the royal presents sent by Vibhishana.

One day the shattering news arrived that Rama had taken jalasamadhi or death by drowning in the river Sarayu. Nikasha went very quiet when she was told of it by a weeping Vibhishana. She went away to prostrate in her prayer room before the sandalwood box holding Rama's letters and contrived to slip out of the palace as she had on the day of that last battle. Making her way to the seashore, she looked at the bridge of boulders on which Rama had crossed with his army to Lanka. What courage and dedication it stood for.

'O Rama, my life came out of its darkness because of you,' she thought. 'I wanted to die after my sons were killed. But strangely, I also wanted to live longer only to know what you would do. I have no wish to live now. But I realize I cannot run away from life. I will live on until my time comes, thinking of you. The thought of you helped me live through my grief. I wanted to be worthy in your eyes even if you knew nothing of what I tried to do. Who will cure me now of the grief of your death?'

Nikasha made her way back to the palace and passed her remaining years in engagement, not seclusion. She did not let go of the purpose she had found to her life in being useful to her people. This lessened her guilt somewhat about having indulged Ravana so much that he crossed all limits, and assuaged her terrible sorrow for the death of her sons, all sacrificed to Ravana's overweening ego. She supported Vibhishana loyally and ran the women's quarters with order and accord. No more were there wild drinking parties and dishevelled women sprawled everywhere as Hanuman had observed when he had made his way into the palace at night, searching for Sita until he finally located her in the Ashoka grove.

In this quiet way, Nikasha made peace with her existence and lived a life of dignity and service until she too died one day, taking Rama's name with her last breath.

10

Nobody's Child

The story of blind Surdas brings tears to even the most indifferent eyes. Modern India has seen four films on him: *Surdas* (1939), *Bhakta Surdas* (1942), *Sant Surdas* (1975) and *Chintamani Surdas* (1988). His verses are widely sung and danced to, and he is an important figure in the Bhakti movement or devotional revolution that began in South India in the seventh century and spread to North India between the fourteenth and seventeenth centuries, advocating a direct relationship with God. Surdas was reportedly born in Sihi village near Delhi in the fifteenth century. The broad facts of his extraordinary life are documented, as are his compositions, including the anthology called *Sur Sagar*. His verses feature in the Guru Granth Sahib. Surdas continues to be an inspiration to modern seekers of spiritual growth.

'Go away, you accursed child!'

Little Surdas, who was six years old and blind, backed away carefully from his mother, Jamuna. He went next to the courtyard where his father, Ramdas, was teaching his brothers their lessons. Guided by the sound of their voices, he sat behind them and began to listen to what his father was saying. Perhaps they would allow him to be with them this time.

But it was not to be.

'Go away, you accursed child!' shouted his father. The little boy choked on a sob and retreated. Abuse and hatred were his lot for being born blind. He was given burnt rotis unlike his sound, whole brothers who were well fed, loved and pampered. They got new clothes on Deepavali, but he did not. All he could remember, every day of his life, were angry voices that berated him for being born blind, a curse on the family. Taking their cue from their aggrieved parents, his brothers tripped him up, beat him and jostled him from one end of Sihi village to the other.

They came after class for Sur. 'We'll teach you to not disturb us again,' said the eldest brother. They pushed and shoved Sur, cuffing him hard on the head, to the village chowk. 'Stay here now. Don't bother coming back! Nobody wants you!' they said in rough, hard voices, and went home.

Sur subsided in a patient, uncomplaining heap, not daring to even cry. An hour went by and suddenly the chowk rang with singing voices and the sound of cymbals and a drum.

It was a band of travelling singers crossing the village. 'O Krishna, dear child, we love you with all our hearts. Come to our homes, Sweet One. Play with us and let us feed you with fresh, white butter and sugar,' they sang.

Sur's heart beat faster. Who were they singing about? Who was this lucky boy? He got up and began to follow them at a distance.

The troupe, of whom there were four, walked on to the outskirts of the next village, singing in snatches. Sur followed them all the way, stumbling occasionally. It was almost evening by now, and the troupe decided to halt under some trees for the night.

Sur came right up to them and stood patiently, waiting for words.

'Who are you, child?' said the troupe leader at last, noticing that the boy was blind.

'My name is Surdas, Uncle. Please will you take me with you?' said Sur.

'Come and eat with us,' said the leader, and Sur happily came forward. He ate the rotis and vegetables that the troupe cooked over a small thorn fire and went to lie down under a tree as told by the leader.

Sur woke up next morning to the sounds of birds chirping. But there were no sounds of human activity. Where was everyone?

'Uncle! Uncle!' he cried but there was no reply. Not wanting to be burdened by him, the troupe had slipped away at the crack of dawn.

Sur wept in terror. He did not know where he was nor did he know which way to go. He stumbled out into the open, weeping.

'Who are you, boy?' said a voice suddenly. It was the voice of a grown-up woman.

When Sur blurted out his story, the woman took him by the hand.

'Come, I will take you to our village headman,' she said and led the small, frightened boy to her village.

The headman was a large-hearted person with small children of his own. He deeply pitied the forlorn scrap of humanity that stood before him.

'I will keep him with me and look after him if you permit,' said the lady unexpectedly, also filled with pity.

'That is very good of you. Please do that,' said the headman approvingly.

A new life began for Sur from that day. First of all, he was not scolded and abused by anybody. Second, he was fed well. Third, the headman gave him his son's old clothes and so he no longer stood in rags. His guardian helped him bathe by the well and gave him proper bedding to sleep on. The village school teacher let him come for lessons without dakshina, the teacher's fee.

In this kindly atmosphere, initially so alien to him, Sur gradually began to pluck up courage. He did not miss his unkind family at all, for there was nothing to miss. However, once in a while, when his friends were lovingly called home by their mothers, his heart would hurt and his eyes prickle with hot tears. At such times, he would instinctively cringe as though expecting a blow and a flow of abuse.

Several years went by and Sur proved surprisingly handy to the villagers. He had some sort of knack or intuition for finding lost things, be it a pickaxe or a buffalo that had strayed. This raised his value in the community. Sur discovered another knack. He could sing and compose verses. Feeling secure in his surroundings, Sur began to sing at the village chowk. People gathered to listen to him and some even began noting his songs down.

All of Sur's songs were about Krishna. He was obsessed with, and even jealous of, this wonderful boy whom everybody loved despite him being a butter thief and playing so many pranks on people. Everybody, just everybody, from small children to great-grandparents, loved Krishna. What made them love Krishna so much long after he was gone when he, Sur, alive in the present, could not get a jot of love from his own mother and father? His heart hurt to think about it.

Sur tried to find out everything he could about Krishna and there was no dearth of people to tell him, from his guardian to the schoolteacher, to visiting kathakars or devotional storytellers who regularly held week-long storytelling sessions at the village temple called 'Bhagvat Saptah'.

Without realizing it, Sur, who was nobody's child, steadily guilt-tripped Krishna in his songs, pointedly calling him 'Nand ke dulare' or 'Nanda's beloved child'. He could not stop thinking about Krishna. The obsession grew with every passing year until one spring, unable to bear it any more, he thought of leaving the village to go look for Krishna and confront him with the injustice of the world. But how could he leave his kind guardian who now depended on him in her increasingly feeble old age?

Stopped by his sense of duty, Sur stayed on for a few more years. But when his guardian died, he felt the old pull pulsing stronger than ever.

'But where will you go to find Krishna? Isn't our village temple good enough?' said the headman.

'I will go to Vrindavan, of course. That is his home,' said Sur stoutly.

'It is quite far away. Let me send someone with you,' said the headman, and so Sur set off with a young man from the village on the road to Vrindavan. They journeyed for several days comfortably enough, but when they came to the Madhuvan forest, Sur's companion, who was homesick, lost heart and left Sur to find his way on his own.

Undaunted, Sur bravely entered the forest. He tripped over roots and stones but did not let the cuts and bruises bother him much. 'Krishna! Krishna!' he chanted and felt about him for the way forward.

Around midday on his third day in the forest, Sur suddenly felt himself falling into a deep hole in the ground. He was unable to climb out. Sur felt afraid for the first time in his journey. It was the same terrifying dread he had once felt as a child. 'Krishna! Krishna!' he called frantically, but nobody seemed to hear him. Sur sat down, worn out.

Suddenly he heard a bright, boyish voice saying, 'Hold up your arms. I will pull you out.'

Sur leapt to his feet and two sturdy young hands took hold of him and pulled him out of the hole.

Breathless with the effort, Sur barely found the voice to say 'Thank you', but there was no answer. The boy had vanished as mysteriously as he had appeared.

Sur called and called until he was hoarse, but it was of no use.

'That was Krishna,' Sur found himself thinking excitedly. 'Did you indeed come for me, Krishna? Who else could it have been? Oh Krishna, why didn't you stay to talk to me? I have so much to ask you.'

Unafraid now, Sur somehow made his way through the forest and soon fell in with groups of people going to Vrindavan.

'Please take me to the biggest Krishna temple here,' said Sur, and the people led him to the Dwarkadhish temple. There, Sur was taken to the presence of a holy man called Swami Vallabhacharya who was a local spiritual leader of great note.

'You have come home now. I will look after you from now on,' said the Swami consolingly after hearing his story.

Sure enough, he gave Sur a comfortable room to stay in, gave him new clothes, a plate and a water-pot of his own, a palmetto fan and other small comforts. He also appointed a minder to show Sur his way around and, best of all, gave Sur a tanpura for his music.

Sur was now set for life. He felt it was his just reward for his heroic efforts to cope with his troubles and happily settled down in Vrindavan under Swami Vallabhacharya's special care. He sang every day in the temple and was greatly appreciated by all who heard him. They too began noting down his songs.

Many years passed this way, and Sur grew old and grey. But he never stopped accusing Krishna of injustice. This was a lingering thorn in his heart, but one day this too was plucked out. It happened this way.

One spring, Sur sat singing on the grass outside the Dwarkadhish temple, enjoying the pleasant morning sunshine. The air was sweet with the scent of flowers. Songbirds chirped and a fresh breeze blew in from the Yamuna. But suddenly, there was a new sound – the unmistakable sound of a child's tinkling anklet bells. Sur stopped to listen.

'How beautifully you sing, do sing more,' said a bright, boyish voice. Memory stirred. 'O Krishna, is that you? Why did you leave me alone all these years?' asked Sur pitifully.

'But I never left you. I came to you so many times. Didn't you recognize me?' said the voice. 'Never mind, do sing another song.'

Sur gulped, nodded and sang with tears pouring down his old, wrinkled face as he quavered, 'Main nahin makhan khaayo, maiyya mori' or 'O mother, it was not I who ate the butter'.

'Thank you,' said the boy in a sweet, mannerly voice.

'Did you really like it?' stammered Sur but there was no

answer. Instead, Sur heard the sound of tinkling anklets fade as the boy got up and went away.

However, realization had split Sur's heart wide open.

'Ah, Krishna, I was unjust to you,' he cried. 'You did indeed come in so many guises to me. But I could not see. You came to me as the travelling singers, as my guardian in the village, as the headman, as my friends, as the boy in the forest, as Swami Vallabhacharya. You are the friendship of friends, the goodness of the good.'

Sur's oldest grudge and bitterest grief, though whittled away somewhat by his better experiences, were resolved at last in his mind. Krishna had come to him in the very form that Sur had addressed him. Sur realized that his old heart had remained that of a hurt and grieving little boy all along and that he felt much better now, and full of gratitude for all the goodness that had come his way. He also felt good that he had kept trying to express himself throughout and had plucked up the nerve to go looking for Krishna in his childhood haunts.

He lived the rest of his life in great peace and happiness, knowing little though that his songs would be sung even centuries later, and his tale would be told and retold as a journey from deepest despair to glorious contentment.

11

The Compromise

The story of Ahalya and Gautama is often narrated as a straightforward tale of crime, punishment and redemption. But the crux of it lies in the complicated relationship of Ahalya and Gautama, and their proud, sensitive son, first found in the Valmiki Ramayana, with layers added over time.

There is an unusual twist in this story of love and loss. Ahalya, or Ahilya, is respected despite her lapse from the stern social code that 'nice women don't'. Moreover, Valmiki's Rama does not do as he is shown to do by later storytellers, that is, place his foot on Ahalya. Not only was the Prince of Ayodhya too respectful towards women to do that, but also Ahalya was not turned to stone in Valmiki's Ramayana.

This well-known story has attracted much disapproving male commentary, but the camps are divided. Some say it was not Ahalya's fault, while others say she knew what she was doing. A third camp avers that her punishment made up for it and after all, she was redeemed and respected by none other than Rama, as presented by Rishi Valmiki, with layers added over time.

'Your mother is dead! Your mother is dead!'

'No, she is not! She will come back one day.'

'Your mother is dead and your father's gone away. You're an orphan, an orphan!'

'No, I'm not. My father will come back, too. And I'm coming for you.'

Saying so, Sadananda hurled himself at his tormentor, another small boy like him, and pummelled him in fury. The boy howled aloud and angry adults came running to separate them.

Sadananda ran away to a corner to shed hot tears of rage. He would show these mean boys. It was not his fault if his mother had been cursed by his father to disappear and his father had retreated to brood in the Himalayas, far away from the gurukul in Mithila. How could he avenge his anger? He was only nine years old and his guru was kind to him, as was Guruma. Only some of his fellow pupils were unkind about his family. He could not bear that. He would show them by the only way open to him, which was to study. He would top his class and leave them far behind. And he would thrash them physically too.

Sadananda felt better after this decision. He began to apply himself earnestly to study and as the months passed, the taunts grew less, for his grim, determined face, his excellence in class and his readiness with his fists gradually discouraged his taunters. You really could not belittle someone like that without consequences.

Invisible among the ashes in her empty home, Ahalya brooded over her plight. She looked sadly at her beautiful hermitage. The large garden was full of shady trees and pleasant nooks. A little stream ran through the grounds with smooth, cool stones on its banks on which one could lie down and tickle the fish. Flowering plants of every kind grew everywhere, and there was a big patch of kusa grass for her husband Gautama's rituals. The ashram was in a forest just outside Mithila city, known as Mithila Upavan. King Janaka was the wise, strong and upright ruler of Mithila. He had four daughters whom he cherished dearly. Ahalya wondered who their husbands would be. She hoped they would be happy.

She had been happy too. Lord Brahma had fashioned her out of everything that was beautiful on earth. He had done this to teach Urvashi a lesson. Urvashi was the chief apsara in Lord Indra's heavenly court and had grown increasingly arrogant. So Brahma had created Ahalya who was even more beautiful. Indra had wanted Ahalya at once but Brahma in his wisdom bestowed her on the great seer Gautama. Gautama was much older than Ahalya but a bull-like man of great strength and vigour. He had performed severe austerities and developed immense yogic powers of body and mind.

He was tender to Ahalya and deeply protective, encouraging her to develop the ashram garden. Ahalya delighted him with her witty ripostes, her silver laughter and her loving nature. They were both ecstatic when their son, Sadananda, was born.

What had gone wrong in this idyll? When had Ahalya turned into a neglected wife? Gautama had plunged into long and deep austerities one year and hardly noticed Ahalya any more. He even stopped playing with Sadananda, so lost was he in his own thoughts. From a happy home filled with love and laughter, the ashram had become a tense, uncomfortable place where only mother and son spoke to each other, until that too ceased when Sadananda, at age eight, was sent to a gurukul in Mithila.

Ahalya went about her chores with a downcast face. One fateful day, Gautama came home early. The water from his bath in the river danced in golden drops on his body. He smiled meaningfully at Ahalya and held out his arms. Ahalya melted gladly into his embrace but as they lay down, she stiffened with shock. There was a new and celestial fragrance on Gautama's body. It could not be Gautama. Who was it then? It could only be Indra. But Ahalya was so lost in the moment that she succumbed.

When Indra got up to leave, Ahalya hastily arranged her clothes and tidied her hair. But what was this? The real Gautama strode up the steps, freshly bathed, with sacred ash marking his mighty limbs. Ahalya and Indra saw him at the same time. Indra panicked, turned himself into a cat and vanished through the window.

'Who was that?' asked Gautama unsuspiciously.

Ahalya's quick wit led her to say, 'majjara'. This meant 'cat' but if split as ma-jara, it meant 'my lover'. So she cleverly avoided lying outright.

But Gautama was not a great yogi for nothing. He could sense a lie straight away. Now he turned his yogic vision on Ahalya and discovered what had just happened. He cursed Indra at once to lose his masculinity. But what was he going to do about Ahalya?

She stood silently before him, looking beseechingly at his stern, angry face.

Gautama looked at her with inner confusion. This was his beautiful bride whom he loved dearly. How could he bear to curse her? They belonged together and he did not want to lose her.

'Have you anything to say?' he asked at last.

'He came disguised as you. I did not realize it until it was too late. I love you. I will always love you and never another. Please forgive me.'

Gautama knew she was being absolutely honest. He had to do something, but what? He decided to buy time.

'Ahalya, I am very hurt by this. I want to go away to the mountains and be by myself, meditating. What am I going to do with you meanwhile? How can you stay here alone and unprotected with me gone? What if that scoundrel comes back? What if you turn weak again? I am going to make you invisible, Ahalya. Stay here among the ashes of our home fires. Your food will be the air. One day, however, Rama, the young prince of Ayodhya, will come this way with Rishi Vishwamitra. I can foresee it. You will regain your form the moment he sets foot in our ashram. I will come back then.'

Ahalya cried aloud and threw herself at Gautama, who held her tight and stroked her hair.

'Farewell, wife. I must go now,' he said after a few moments, and as he turned, Ahalya became invisible.

Ahalya's days seemed unending to her. Although invisible to others, she felt alive and normal, though devoid of hunger and thirst. She bathed in the stream and tended to the garden as before. But the house wore a neglected look, for there were no hearth fires burning and no family life to give it a lived-in appearance. Ahalya made a small Shivlinga with mud near the stream and offered it flowers and water every morning. She spent hours before it, meditating on Shiva and Parvati. 'You have a complicated relationship, too. Yet, you are an example of married love to everyone else,' she said wonderingly. She thought of her son every day and prayed for his welfare. She missed him and missed her husband very much.

'I am suffering because I made him suffer,' she thought sorrowfully of Gautama. 'I will make it up to him when he comes back. Meanwhile, I can give my life purpose through prayer. It cleanses my mind and fills my days with meaning. But O Rama, when will you come and set me free?'

~

Years went by and Ahalya tried her best to work out her long penance, following a routine of gardening, prayer and meditation. Despite her quick wit and her creativity, her skill as a gardener, and above all, her incandescent beauty, she was a humble, straightforward person who loved her little family and felt deeply disgraced by what had befallen her.

'Everyone knows that I have been cursed by my husband to be invisible until the appointed day. Oh, the shame of it. Though King Janaka promised my husband that nobody would violate the ashram in his absence, Sadananda never comes here. My little son, how I long to see you and hold you. A million curses on Indra. What did I ever do to harm anyone that I was picked on like this? My husband, don't forsake me. My happiness is with you. Please come back soon. O Prince Rama, when will you come to redeem me?'

Such unhappy thoughts tortured poor Ahalya daily and left her weeping by the stream. Invisible to the eye, she would pick herself up morosely after each bout of tears and tend to her plants. This gave her some comfort. But the changing seasons tormented her for she longed to cook for her husband and son as the fruits and vegetables came and went in the ashram garden. The flowers made her long to braid them in garlands for the household gods, and the grasses made her want to plait new mats and baskets for her home.

Meanwhile, Sadananda shone at studies and earned a very good reputation. His intellectual prowess and spiritual lustre came to the notice of King Janaka of Mithila, and by and by, Sadananda was appointed to the high office of Rajguru, or royal priest. He conducted all the rituals and ceremonies of royal life with great effectiveness. The gods smiled on Mithila, pleased with its prayers and offerings. But in his heart of hearts, Sadananda was a grieving boy still, yearning to see his parents. He never attempted to visit his childhood home though, for he could not bear to go there while his mother lay under a curse.

One day, as foreseen by Gautama, Rishi Vishwamitra escorted Rama and Lakshmana, the princes of Ayodhya, to Mithila. He was taking them to King Janaka's court to see the great bow of Shiva kept there as a treasured relic. As they walked through the forest outside Mithila, Rama noticed Ahalya's hermitage.

'Whose is this lovely ashram, Gurudev?' he asked Vishwamitra. 'It looks so beautiful, but there is no plume of smoke. It seems to be uninhabited. How is it possible?'

'It is empty because of a great seer's anger,' said Vishwamitra and told the princes the story of Ahalya.

'Now let us enter the hermitage and put an end to the torture of penitent Ahalya,' said Vishwamitra, leading the way.

As soon as Rama set foot in the ashram grounds, a great light seemed to blaze and Ahalya appeared in it, like the full moon coming out of the clouds. Her beauty shone golden and her smile and graceful namaste were charming beyond belief.

Rama went forward and touched her feet respectfully. As Ahalya gave him the customary blessing, flowers rained down on them from the celestials. They were pleased and thankful for her restitution since Indra's disgrace reflected poorly on them, too.

Rishi Gautama suddenly appeared by his yogic power, and Ahalya greeted him joyfully. She invited the two rishis and the princes to sit in the garden while she readied her home to receive them. She offered them cool water to drink from the stream and plucked berries and fruit from the garden that she served on a hastily washed wooden platter that she found lying in the ashes.

After spending some time together in good fellowship, Vishwamitra and the princes left for Mithila. Their last glimpse of the ashram was of Gautama and Ahalya standing together at the gate, radiating strength and beauty as though they were Shiva and Parvati themselves.

When they reached the outskirts of Mithila, King Janaka, accompanied by his ministers and Sadananda, came out to welcome them warmly. Vishwamitra told Janaka about the princes and related what had just taken place at Gautama's ashram. Sadananda was greatly excited when he heard this. He looked gratefully at Rama and thanked him for ending his mother's long suffering.

King Janaka gave him leave to go home and Sadananda left at once. He had not seen his parents for over fifteen years and despite his learning and great tapas, felt overcome by tears. He would go home and fill his starved heart with the sight of his reunited parents.

After a gloriously happy week spent at home with his mother and father, Sadananda returned to his duties at Mithila. His respect for his mother was unbounded, for not only had she accepted her lot without protest but also had spent her grieving penance trying to make the best of it, not the worst. Watching his parents with adult eyes, Sadananda realized that their bond was unbreakable and that each had tried to keep hold of the other in their own way. They would live in precious, companionable togetherness now. Feeling whole again, Sadananda set forth to live his own life, at peace with himself.

12

Which Way Forward?

Tukaram was born in Dehu village, near modern-day Pune, in the seventeenth century. Although there is a lot of devotional folklore about him, there is broad consensus that he was overcome by personal tragedies and professional failure. However, the common people grew to love him, and he stands tall even today as a dearly beloved person who struggled to remake his life meaningfully after many setbacks.

Tukaram continues to affect modern Indians deeply. In the 2005 play *Dark Horse*, about the twentieth-century Marathi poet Arun Kolatkar, a journalist asks Kolatkar if he believes in God. The poet takes his time to answer, and finally says, 'Well, I know Tukaram, and Tukaram knows God.' The Marathi film *Sant Tukaram* (1936) was the first Indian film to get international recognition, when it was adjudged one of the three best films in the world in 1937 at the Venice Film Festival. Tukaram's living legacies are his abhangs or devotional compositions, which are very popular not only in his home state Maharashtra, but across South India. Carnatic musicians regularly sing his songs, which have acquired cult status.

'I can't believe how stupid you are!'

'You let your family die. You don't have a heart.'

'Are you a grown man or an infant?'

'You are manda-buddhi, mentally deficient!'

Tukaram shrank into himself as the harsh words of his business friends and neighbours fell on him like hail. Had the world no mercy and pity?

The year was 1630 and a terrible famine had wrecked Maharashtra. Tukaram's frail wife, Rukma, and his eldest son had just died in it. Tukaram's parents, Bolhoba and Kankai, had died five years earlier and his elder brother, Savaji, had left home to become a sanyasi, a wandering mendicant. Tuka, who had inherited a prosperous family shop selling grain, spices and cloth, had run his business into the ground in 1629 with his soft heart, giving things away freely and not managing his affairs with acumen. He was nearly destitute the next year when the famine took hold and could not buy his family either food or medicine.

When he returned from their cremation, the world was waiting to fall on him with reproaches and recriminations.

Tuka did not know what to say to them. He was only twenty-one years old, having been married off early, as was the custom. He folded his hands in namaste, tears running down his face. Satisfied, his tormentors went away.

What should he do now? Where was his life headed? He could not think of an answer and went and sat desolately at the household shrine, grieving for his lost ones.

'Vithoba. Krishna,' he breathed, at the sight of the family deity whose temple lay in Pandharpur, on the banks of the gracefully curving river Chandrabhaga. Here, in his native village of Dehu by the river Indrayani, Tuka felt his heart leap with sudden longing for Pandharpur. He was no stranger to it for his parents had been fervent devotees of Vithoba and had taken him with them on their pilgrimages twice a year, in the months of Asadh (June–July) and Kartik (October–November).

He decided to go there the very next day. Avali, his second wife, silently fed him some cold rice and salted buttermilk, which stayed his hunger until morning. She kept their surviving children quiet by force of will, and too cowed and miserable to rebel, they went to sleep. Tuka's younger brother Kanhoba made himself scarce.

~

Tuka thought of his mother, Kankai, on his way to Pandharpur, and of the great saints of the region like Pundalik, Namdev and Chokhamela. He thought of his ancestor Vishwambhar who had loved Vithoba dearly and guided by a dream, had found an idol of Vithoba at Dehu. But especially, he thought of his mother. Kankai had loved Vithoba with all her heart and soul. And when she was expecting Tuka, an even deeper fervour had seized her. She withdrew from all social life and was indifferent to household chores, mechanically performing just enough. She spent her time looking at birds and butterflies, and trees and plants, weaving flower garlands for Vithoba, praying and meditating.

'No wonder my feet are drawn to Vithoba,' thought Tuka as he trudged along. 'I was in my mother's body then, absorbing everything she felt.'

Pandharpur.

Tuka's heart leapt at the sight. He ran forward to the temple and hastily washing his hands and feet, went in and threw himself down at the idol's feet. 'Vithoba, guide me, please. My life is shattered. My first wife, Rukma, and eldest son, Narayan, are dead. My other wife nags me all the time. I have five other mouths to feed, counting my younger brother. Can I blame Avali for being impatient? She was a rich grocer's daughter. I was forcibly married a second time because Rukma fell ill so often. I have bankrupted my business and made Avali wretched, too. What a failure I am. Everyone I know jeers at me. How should I go forward now?'

The dark, glowing image of Vithoba on his brick, arms akimbo, seemed to shimmer before Tuka's eyes. A dancing, singing band of pilgrims entered the shrine just then. By and by, one of them pulled Tuka to his feet.

'Dance with us, brother! Don't you know that Vithoba joins in when we dance for him? Can you not sense him in our midst?'

As Tuka danced to the energetic rhythm, he felt renewed and hopeful.

'I will be true to myself, Vithoba, with your song in my heart and on my lips. I will not try to be cleverer than I am.'

Tuka went home to Dehu, feeling somewhat better about his decision. There he found that Avalibai had pledged her remaining ornaments and raised 250 rupees for him to start a new business with. Tuka thanked her for her loyalty and set off to Baleghat with a supply of salt to sell.

Having sold his goods, Tuka was walking back to Dehu when he fell in with a poor and visibly depressed man. Being Tuka, he immediately asked the man his trouble. Out came a pathetic story of debtors who could not be paid for lack of money. Impulsively, Tuka gave the stranger everything he had.

When he got home to Dehu, Avali's rage and stupefaction were nothing compared to the fury of the public. The neighbours declared Tuka insane. They hung a garland of onions on his neck, forcibly seated him on a donkey and paraded him through the village, beating drums and jeering.

This humiliation pushed Tuka to the brink. His grief and rage threatened to burst his heart.

He called a family conference that evening.

'I am useless as a businessman. I have failed you and now I wish to go away. I will write the house in Kanhoba's name.

Avali, I know your father will welcome you back although he will be displeased with me. But neither you nor I had a choice about marriage, did we? You won't starve, nor will the children. I set you free honourably. I will leave tomorrow.'

His family wept inconsolably but finally accepted his decision.

Tukaram was still in his early twenties then. Shy and tender-hearted but also proud, he acknowledged that he was a misfit in his society and in his profession. He renounced the world and left home to meditate on the nearby hillside of Bhambhanath, taking only a few necessary things with him.

Over the years, Avali and Kanhoba got on fairly well with their lives, and so did Tuka. Avali's suddenly single status was excused by the fact that her husband had turned to saintly pursuits. Her father, though embarrassed at first to have a married daughter returned to him as neither a wife nor a widow, gave in to his natural affection and made Avali and her children feel welcome. Kanhoba took over the derelict family store and made it prosperous, being both practical and shrewd.

As for Tuka, he lived out several years in voiceless fury and grief at how very wrong his life had gone. 'I started with everything, but I was left with nothing because of my trusting, foolish nature. I am a failure as a businessman, a husband and a parent. But was I ever given a choice? It was the world that made me a businessman and a family man and then blamed me when I didn't get it right. It made fun of me and punished me. I cannot bear it. I have nobody but God now,' he berated himself daily. He thought of frail Rukma and how she had begged him to marry Avali since she was too weak to bear him children. He thought of Avali's loyalty and affection. He thought of his son Narayan growing weaker by the day and dying in his arms. The faces of his remaining children and his brother appeared in an indistinguishable blur to him. Did he really love them?

This thought set off a new round of grief that his heart was incapable of accommodating natural ties beyond a point.

'I find my family uninteresting. I find more pleasure in God,' he thought, startled. 'Am I unnatural? Am I selfish? How can I deny that I feel much happier alone on the hillside than at home with its constant clamour or the shop with its endless petty sums?'

As he progressed from shame and grief to accepting the truth of his feelings, Tukaram began to live in a sort of ecstasy on the hillside, relieved to have shaken off the earthly bonds that were not of his choosing but imposed on him by the norms of his society. 'I have found myself in Vithoba,' he thought gratefully and sang of his love. Everybody, he sang, belonged to God, and God in turn belonged to them. You could see Vithoba in every leaf and flower, in every bird and butterfly. Vithoba was the only reality that mattered.

Stopping at first in ones and twos, and gradually gathering in a crowd to hear him sing, the shepherds, carpenters, weavers and ploughmen of the village found a strange joy in Tuka's simple but moving songs. Their hard lives suddenly seemed less hard to them and they became more aware of the beauty of creation, of which they now felt that they, too, were a part. They fed Tukaram enough food to keep him going, rustic meals offered with love. Tuka hardly noticed what it was but ate with gratitude.

As word spread, people from other villages came just to listen to the singing saint on the hillside. People showed up with ink and palm leaves and noted down his compositions. The songs passed from lip to lip in no time at all, and many people came to know of his songs. They were called 'abhang', meaning 'unbroken', signifying that God's songs are unbreakable and eternal. Tuka was touched and pleased when his listeners joined in the singing, having memorized his words.

The seasons seemed to fly by, unnoticed, and with every year Tuka's hunger to reach the Lord's lotus feet grew stronger. His longing to meet Vithoba, from being a joyous urge, became a source of sorrow to him that deepened every day. Why was it taking so long? His songs grew abstract and philosophical about the indwelling God who also contained the universe.

One day, at the age of forty-two, almost half a life after his renunciation, Tuka could not wait any longer. 'God, I have tried my best all these years. I am so tired. I cannot wait to see you. I am coming to you now. Do not refuse me,' he said piteously. He bid farewell to the hillside and laying aside his water-pot, rug, cymbals and lute, made his way down to the river Indrayani, trembling in excitement.

'Hari, Hari,' his blood seemed to sing in him and the river

tugged gently at his limbs as if to say, 'Come with me, I will take you where you want to go.' Tuka waded in deeper and deeper, chanting Vithoba's name until the cool green waters closed over his head. He smiled in bliss as he sank into the river's embrace and was never seen again.

But the people remembered and never forgot. Tuka was a success after all, in a way that would have brought his soul peace.

13

Baiju the Insane

Most people say that the legend of Baiju Bawra or 'Baiju the Insane' is a myth. There was a Hindi film about him in 1952 that is considered complete fiction, although it was a huge hit and its songs are evergreen. Whatever be the facts of the case, a story has persisted in India since the fifteenth or sixteenth century and come down to us in the twenty-first century about a classical singer of that name in North India who went through many trials and tribulations. Historical figures appear in some versions of the legend.

Baiju, according to tradition, learnt music from Swami Haridas, a real person, and an important composer and spiritual leader. Swami Haridas was a direct disciple of Purandara Dasa, the 'Karnataka Sangita Pitamaha' or the Father of Carnatic Music. There is a Swami Haridas Sangeet Sammelan or commemorative classical music festival held every year in Mumbai since 1952 and so, in a reversal of the norm, Baiju is also remembered through his guru.

Sometime in the fifteenth or sixteenth century, Baiju, or Baijnath, was the spoilt only son of a poor but happy couple in Champaner in the Gujarat Sultanate. But when his father took ill and died, there was neither home nor money to be had. Baiju's mother took him with her to Vrindavan, the traditional refuge of the destitute. How they made the long, dusty journey to the banks of the Yamuna was an ordeal that only the migrant poor could understand – the weary, cracked feet, the thirst, the hunger, the fear of attack, the agony of tramping mile after mile on the endless road. It took them more than a month, but they did it at last.

A poorhouse in Krishna's holy city took them in, and so the urgent needs of food and shelter were met. But how were they to live? The poorhouse provided a morning meal and a smaller evening meal. But what about money for clothes, and how were they to pay for Baiju's education? Baiju's father had been a scholar and Baiju's mother, though used to a simple life on his meagre earnings, was proud of her husband and mourned him sincerely. She was determined that Baiju should learn his letters. She asked around and gamely took employment as a servant in the house of a rich seth, or merchant, family. The wages were fair and her employers were kind, so Baiju's mother plucked up the courage to ask for advice on Baiju's schooling. The patriarch of the house recommended a small gurukul some distance away. So with a sense of relief, Baiju's mother had him admitted there.

Baiju went off to school humming. He liked to sing and often sang the little songs his mother taught him. As he walked down the lanes, he suddenly heard the most glorious singing. Baiju could not move at first. He made his way to the house where the music was coming from and peeped into the outer courtyard. A man was seated there plucking a stringed instrument, singing loudly with his eyes closed. Baiju could not help himself. He walked in and sat cross-legged on the ground before the singer to hear him properly.

The singer opened his eyes when the song ended.

'Did you like the song?' he asked Baiju cordially.

Baiju nodded vigorously. 'I want to sing like you,' he said with childish directness.

'Why don't you sing something you know?' invited the man.

Baiju launched at once into a Krishna bhajan that his mother had taught him.

The man looked at him in delight.

'I will teach you, little one. Bring your father to see me.'

'I will bring my mother,' said Baiju, and did so next morning.

And so began the most magical nine years for Baiju.

His teacher, Swami Haridas, was not only a great singer

but also a composer and a holy man with many followers. He had offered to teach Baiju on a kindly whim because of the boy's simplicity and good voice. This was a great piece of luck for Baiju although he was too young to realize it then. He went to music class early in the morning, to gurukul after that for reading, writing and arithmetic and back to music class after school.

For over a year, Swami Haridas set Baiju to study the first musical note 'sa'. It was called 'shadja grama' or 'the domain of sa'. In it lay all music. Swami Haridas then initiated him into the mystery and rigour of the song form called dhrupad.

'It comes from the Sama Veda itself and is described in the oldest book on art theory, the *Natya Shastra*,' taught the Swami. 'It has four parts that you gradually enter and build up and must learn to leave gracefully at the end. We also call the dhrupad "Vishnu Pada", the Lord's metre.'

Baiju drank it all in eagerly. He also learnt to play the stringed lute that his guru played, the rudra veena. A pakhawaj drum maestro from the holy city of Nathdwara was Swami Haridas's in-house accompanist, and he taught Baiju the principles and practice of percussion. As his skill and musicality began to improve, Baiju felt enabled to sing for hours, exploring the shades and nuances of the mighty ragas that the Swami led him into.

It was not long before Baiju became famous as a musician in Vrindavan. His singing attracted huge crowds, and the big temples began to invite him to perform. This was a great honour, for the temples were the cultural hub of society where nritya seva, or dance, and sangeet seva, or music, were regularly performed as activities that were greatly pleasing to the gods.

When Baiju turned eighteen, his mother found him a sweet-natured bride, and two children, a boy and a girl, were born to him. Gone were the days of poverty and deprivation. Baiju bought a little house with his concert fees, and his mother no longer went to work. Invitations to sing poured in from neighbouring towns, and he was invited to perform at the important royal courts of Chanderi and Gwalior. Baiju's career was at an all-time high. Life was blissful and family life was sweetest of all.

One day, an exciting invitation showed up in the form of a royal messenger. The maharaja of a Himalayan kingdom wanted Baiju to be his court singer. A big fee was promised and as proof of faith, the maharaja had sent silk, gold and jewels to Baiju along with the invitation.

Baiju could not resist the temptation. His family was in tears about his going away, but Baiju overrode them in his excitement. 'I will be back in no time at all,' he laughed and left the very next day with the messenger, not even taking leave of his guru.

~

Ten dizzy, wonderful years passed before Baiju felt even remotely homesick. The Himalayan maharaja made him very welcome and presented him with robes of honour. He grew very attached to Baiju and took him everywhere with him. He invited neighbouring royals to special concerts to show off Baiju as an ornament of his court. Lost in the glamour and ceremony, Baiju emotionally disowned his past and lived for the day, vastly enjoying himself.

One day, however, he suddenly found himself thinking of his family. After many pleas, he was allowed by the maharaja to go back to Vrindavan. Baiju hurried home with great scenes playing in his mind of how his family would be overjoyed to see him.

But a terrible shock awaited him in Vrindavan. His house no longer existed, having been pulled down and remade into the annexe of a neighbouring house. There was absolutely no sign of his family. Baiju went from house to house asking for them, but there were many new people in the lane and nobody could answer him. The shopkeepers nearby did not know. Finally, an old maidservant in one of the houses vaguely recalled that the family had gone away years ago. She did not know where.

Clueless and frustrated, Baiju finally thought of going to his guru's house. But another shock awaited him there. Swami Haridas had passed away. The people there were cold to Baiju, remembering his sudden, thankless disappearance. They knew nothing about his family.

Baiju could not bear the shock and the guilt.

He made his way dazedly to the temples where he had once been an honoured artist, but nobody could tell him anything.

'If you disappear for a decade, do you expect time to stand still here in Vrindavan?' said a priest pointedly.

Baiju cried loudly at that. He felt as though his heart would burst. Weeping bitterly, he made his way into the kunj gali or lanes of Vrindavan, not knowing where to go. He slept under a tree by the Yamuna and woke up without a plan.

One day passed, and then another, and Baiju rapidly deteriorated into an unhinged state of mind. He lived off scraps from the temples. His clothes wore thin and his hair grew wild and unkempt. He soon looked like a beggar and wandered all day around Vrindavan, accosting startled pilgrims to ask, 'Have you seen my family? Tell me where they are.' The pilgrims withdrew hastily from him.

Soon, Baiju began to be called 'bawra', or 'insane', in Vrindavan. He babbled incessantly of his family and burst into sudden bouts of weeping. Nobody wanted to have anything to do with him.

Baiju sat for hours alone by the Yamuna reproaching himself for his neglect of his family. 'I was vain and stupid. I let go of them. Mother, forgive me!' he wept, unable to deal coherently with his grief.

One day, as Baiju wandered aimlessly around town, his feet strayed down the lane where his guru had once lived. As he passed his guru's house, he heard the sound of singing. Several former students of Swami Haridas had gathered to sing his compositions. The Swami had composed two kinds of songs. The 'siddhanta pada' were deeply philosophical. The 'keli mala', or 'garland of play', chronicled the sport of

Krishna and Radha, giving full agency to Radha, describing her as equal, and even superior, to Krishna.

'Two beams of light play, unequalled in their dance and music,' went the song, and Baiju walked into the courtyard to listen as he had done all those years ago.

The music broke through the dark misery that clouded his mind. He recalled how his guru had taught him this very song. He sat up straight and began to really listen. Hesitantly at first but soon with full-throated power, he joined in the singing. There was a ripple of surprise, but the singing went on unabated. Baiju sang every song with them. After some time, the singers paused and invited him to sing alone.

Tears filled Baiju's eyes as he thought of his guru and he sang his heart out for nearly an hour. His audience was deeply moved. When the singing was done, they begged him to stay on in the Swami's house, which was now run by his disciples as a home for musicians.

This marked the beginning of Baiju's long recovery. He had his hair cut and he started to bathe every day again. The Swami's disciples, his guru bhai or 'brothers in study', gave him two sets of simple clothes, one to wash and one to wear. Food was no longer an issue. Baiju went to sleep at night in deep gratitude.

'I have been given a second chance by my guru's grace. I must try now to pay my dues,' he thought.

This transition from borderline insanity to steady, normal behaviour was not easy. Baiju felt his heart heave painfully whenever thoughts of his family came back. He would sit in a corner weeping until the fit of agony passed. He learnt to ride the waves of grief, not attempting to resist them but to weep as he was swept along, and empty his heart. After the bout subsided, he washed his face and tried to make himself useful in some way in the guru's house.

He helped fetch water and kindling for the kitchen fires. He polished the copper and brass vessels and lamps with ashes from the kitchen, shining them up to a high degree of brilliance. He helped pick the rice and dal clean, knead the dough and chop the vegetables. No task was too low or beneath his dignity. Gone were the days of brocade coats and jewelled bracelets. With the same childlike simplicity that he had gone to Swami Haridas's and forgotten his family for ten years, Baiju now forgot all about the glittering life he had led as a court musician. He lived for the day once more, immersed in his singing and finding satisfaction in simple household tasks that made him feel he was part of a family again.

This new humility and sorrow began to be reflected in his singing, which became intensely full of feeling. His listeners found themselves in tears one moment, light and happy the next and full of divine ecstasy at other times. His singing left such an impact on people that they began to say things like 'He could light lamps singing Raag Deepak if he wanted to', and 'He could make it rain singing Raag Megh Malhar if he chose'. These compliments soon turned into folklore and many people actually thought that such supernatural events had been accomplished by Baiju.

One day, an invitation to sing arrived from his old patron, the Raja of Chanderi. Delighted to renew the tie, Baiju set off with the king's messenger. But along the way, he drank some infected water and came down with typhoid. Shaking with fever and nausea, Baiju arrived in a wretched state at Chanderi. The raja immediately had him put in comfortable quarters and attended to by his own vaid, or doctor.

But it was too late to save Baiju. He died on Basant Panchami day when spring was in bloom and the air was soft and scented. He did not grudge going though, for his heart was finally at peace with his efforts to climb out of the darkness.

14

Why Me?

The tale of Nala and Damayanti is a frightening account of how the malevolent fates inflict grief and loss on innocent people. It is found in several books, including the Mahabharata, where Rishi Markandeya tells the story to Yudhishthira in the Kamyaka Forest. In its verse form, in the twelfth-century Naishada Charita by Sriharsha, it is considered one of the five great epic poems in Sanskrit literature and is retold and danced across India to this day. Movies have been based on it, and it served as inspiration for several of Raja Ravi Varma's famous paintings.

The story is a testament to the never-say-die human spirit and to the importance of having interests and developing skills. 'Be engaged' and 'Don't give up easily' are the mottoes of this ancient tale, which probably explains its enduring appeal.

Nala was the king of the Nishadas and as dashing, brave and handsome as one could wish. The gods of Indralok would even seek his help to vanquish demons that they themselves could not defeat. In those days, there was easy traffic between heaven and earth, and the gods walked freely among men. They praised Nala as a perfect hero, as did his loyal subjects, for Nala was a just king. He had only one royal vice, which was gambling. His cousin, Pushkara, excelled in it, whereas Nala played for fun and was not particularly good with the dice.

The public was also intrigued by the range of his interests, both indoor and outdoor ones. Nala was a herbalist who knew the uses of every plant and tree. He was a skilled charioteer who was wise in the way of horses and machines. He could fix a chariot when it developed a fault or a tremor. When a mare foaled in his stables, he did not leave it to the grooms and horse doctor but helped the mare through the birth himself.

His other great interest was food. The palace cooks were praised, encouraged and even personally guided, for Nala himself taught them new recipes and how to improve old ones. 'Food is the gift of the gods. We must cherish it,' he said, and not content with mere talk, he sat down after court duty and hunting to write the first-ever cookbook known to the land, the *Paaka Darpanam*, or 'A Mirror to Cuisine'. This created a sensation when copies were made and presented to the public as well as to the ambassadors from neighbouring kingdoms. In the book, Nala charmingly thanked his mother and maternal uncles for having initiated him into the culinary arts.

'He is so talented,' sighed the noble matrons of Nishada, and threw their daughters at him like a hail of pumpkins, but to no avail. In his secret heart, Nala was a romantic. He wanted to fall deeply in love and be loved back as intensely, like Urvashi and Pururavas, like Atri and Anasuya, and – greatest of all – like Shiva and Parvati.

One day when Nala was out hunting, he found a beautiful swan by a forest pool. He was about to shoot it when the swan spoke in a human voice. 'Don't shoot, king. I am a celestial swan, and you will only create bad karma for yourself by killing me.'

Nala put down his bow and arrow, amazed.

'Thank you,' said the swan. 'I will tell you about Princess Damayanti in return. She is the daughter of King Bheema of Vidarbha, which lies to the south of your kingdom. I have flown everywhere but never have I seen such beauty. I have spent several days quietly observing her. She is intelligent and good natured, well spoken to high and low. She likes to read and sings very well; in fact, she has a beautiful voice. One could listen to it all day and not be wearied. Her father will soon hold a svayamvara for her and invite all the eligible kings so that she can choose a worthy husband.'

Nala's eyes lit up. 'Will you do me a kind favour?' he said. 'Will you fly to Vidarbha and tell the princess about me?'

'I will do it right away,' promised the swan and flew off.

The swan found Damayanti plucking jasmines in the

royal garden. It flew to her and began to speak in a soft voice. Astonished, the princess listened quietly as the swan described Nala of the Nishadas to her. She went back deeply impressed.

That evening when her father discussed her svayamvara with her mother, Damayanti told them about Nala. 'I will invite him, too,' promised her fond father.

But when the great day arrived, there was a shock in store for Damayanti. The gods had decided to come as well, for everyone wanted to win Damayanti for himself. Indra, Vayu, Agni, Yama and Varuna, each laid claim to her by virtue of their divine status.

Damayanti thought hard and spoke her mind.

'I am honoured by your kind attention, O immortals,' she said. 'But I have accepted King Nala of the Nishadas as my husband in my heart. Please let me marry him.'

The gods laughed. 'Not so easily, Damayanti,' said Indra. 'We will all stand in a row with Nala. You must pick him out from amongst us.'

The gods lined up with Nala and, to Damayanti's great fright, they all looked exactly like Nala. Which one was he? She looked again, carefully.

'I must look through to the real person underneath,' she thought. 'It is our very humanity that will let us find each other. The celestials are too perfect, their eyes don't blink, their feet don't quite touch the ground, and they have no signs of dust or sweat on them. Whereas, for all his skills, Nala is just another human being like me.'

Damayanti stepped forward confidently after this observation and garlanded Nala. They were sent off happily after the ceremonies to Nishada.

Meanwhile, the disappointed gods trooped home. On the way, they met Kali, the chief of the demigod Gandharvas, who was on his way to the svayamvara.

'Too late. She has married Nala,' jeered the gods and went their way. Kali felt choked with spite and spleen. 'I won't let them be,' he thought savagely.

Kali could do nothing for twelve years since there was nothing unjust or incorrect in Nala's behaviour. He and Damayanti lived very happily together and had two lovely children, a son, Indra, and a daughter, Indrasena. But one day, Nala made a slight error of judgement in a public case that had come up for hearing. His dharma meter dipped due to that and Kali found a hold at last. He took over Nala's better sense and lit the urge in him to gamble.

Nala got into a game of dice with Pushkara that very week. Kali loaded the dice, and there was no way that inexpert Nala could win. The stakes were the usual in high-powered royal games. Whoever won took the other's kingdom. Within an hour of intense play, Nala was kingdomless and homeless.

Informed of the results, Damayanti acted swiftly. She sent Indra and Indrasena away to her parents in Vidarbha in the care of a trusted charioteer and maid. Unafraid now, she met a shamefaced Nala with a bright smile and said in her sweet voice, 'Let us go, husband.'

Pushkara, out of spite, issued orders that no one should

help the exiled king and queen in any way. So they made their way alone on foot through the city, theirs no more, and into the jungle, numb with shock at how quickly their fate had altered.

Damayanti's delicate feet soon began to bleed on the thorny jungle path and Nala made her sit down while he went to find water. As he bent over a stream with a folded leaf for a cup, Kali took the form of a crow and plucked away Nala's dhoti. He flew off with it, leaving Nala naked. Nala went back in shame to Damayanti who did not say a word. Instead, she tore her sari in two and gave one half silently to Nala, knotting the other half around herself. The exhausted and depressed pair lay down to sleep on the jungle floor.

Nala could not sleep out of distress. 'I have let down Damayanti and my children,' he thought, drowning in shame. The influence of Kali in his mind turned his shame into reckless self-pity. 'I must go away, I can't face Damayanti,' he thought foolishly and crept away into the jungle while she slept, unthinking of what she would feel when she woke up, and the dangers of leaving a beautiful young woman alone in the forest.

Damayanti went into deep shock in the morning when she realized that she had been abandoned. 'Nala, how could you?' she wept. 'I could have gone back to my parents with the children. But I chose instead to go with you in your trouble. Now I must find my way somehow to Vidarbha. But Chedi lies next to Nishada. I must get there first.'

Damayanti knew that Chedi and Vidarbha lay to the

south. Ascertaining which way was east by observing the sun, she began to move in a southerly direction, hoping to exit the jungle and reach habitation.

Nala, meanwhile, wandered deeper and deeper into the jungle, when he suddenly saw something burning. Rushing forward, he saw that a magnificent snake was caught in a small forest fire. Nala ran instinctively to save the snake and pulled it out of the flames. He managed to put out the fire with a stout broken branch and looked for cooling herbs to put on the snake.

The snake lay still under his ministering hands and finally spoke. 'O Nala, you are a good man. Let me thank you.' It leapt suddenly at Nala and bit him deeply with its poisoned fangs. Choking and coughing, Nala began to vomit. It took ten whole minutes before he felt better. But something terrible had happened to him. He was now a misshapen dwarf and no longer his tall, handsome self. He looked at the snake with horror.

'Do not be afraid, Nala. I have expelled the evil gandharva Kali from inside you with my poison. You have vomited him out. Did you know that it was he who made you want to gamble and loaded the dice so that you lost? It was because he wanted your wife for himself.'

'That's unbelievable and terrible! Who are you and why have you changed my appearance?'

'I am Karkotaka Naga, the king of the serpents. I know what goes on in the three worlds. Now listen to me, Nala. This disguise is to conceal your identity. You will regain your form the day you are reunited with your wife. But that will take some effort. Go at once to King Rituparna of Ayodhya. He is a mathematical genius, and gambling is like child's play for him. Join his service as his charioteer and learn about dice from him. Go back with that knowledge to Pushkara, and win your kingdom back. The path to Ayodhya lies this way.'

The serpent vanished with a mighty hiss, and Nala was left to make his way to Ayodhya.

Meanwhile, Damayanti fell in with a group of ascetics who were crossing the jungle on their way to the kingdom of Chedi. They escorted her to the doors of the royal palace where Damayanti boldly demanded to meet the queen. Hesitant at first because of her dishevelled appearance, the guards gave in to her steady, sober manner of speech and sent word inside that Damayanti of Nishada wanted an audience with Queen Bhanumati.

To their great surprise, Queen Bhanumati herself came hurrying out to receive Damayanti, for she was her aunt, her father's sister. After keeping Damayanti with her for a few restorative days, the queen sent Damayanti back by chariot to her parents in Vidarbha loaded with clothes, jewels and presents for Damayanti's parents. Back again in Vidarbha, Damayanti hugged her children hard with tears in her eyes. 'I promise you that I'll find your father,' she said, kissing them. Her anxious parents asked her what she had in mind, and Damayanti discussed a plan that she had been quietly formulating.

With her father's active support, Damayanti sent messengers and scouts in every direction to look for Nala. Each messenger was instructed to ask a coded question that Damayanti knew only Nala could answer.

Being clever at word games and telling stories, she kept herself busy thereafter with her children. But her shattering experience also made her seek out other abandoned women in Vidarbha and set up a home for them, so that they could live with dignity instead of being poor relations and household drudges. She linked the home with the office of the royal tentmaker, so that the women could earn an income through regular sewing and, in tribute to Nala, trained those who were interested as expert cooks. She used Nala's cookbook, of which her parents had a copy, to teach them so they could earn their living as cooks in the homes of the nobility and tradesmen.

Meanwhile, Nala made his way to King Rituparna's court and offered his services. His name, he said, was Bahuka, and he could fix any chariot and drive any horse. After a doubtful look at his appearance, the king decided to give Nala a chance and was delighted with his expertise. He engaged him on the spot and very soon made him his personal charioteer.

It was hard for Nala, a king, to become a servant, but his grief over losing Damayanti and his children drove him on. He tried to stoically put up with the rough company of stable hands and their rude food, thinking, 'This is my penance. It is also a chance for me to learn how common people live and think, so that I can be a better king when I get back my kingdom.' This thought, however, threw him into a new cycle of shame at losing his kingdom and fear of never getting it back. His nights were uneasy and full of tormented thoughts.

Several months passed and King Rituparna grew more and more delighted with Nala. Not only was he a master of all things equine, as promised, but also genuinely knew every last thing about chariots. His manners were polished and his speech refined, although he was short, squat and misshapen. The king dropped his guard with Nala and spoke to him with increasing confidence and trust.

When he felt it was a suitable time to ask, Nala respectfully questioned the king on the art of dice. Amused, Rituparna offered to exchange knowledge. 'You teach me your skill with horses, and I'll teach you everything about dice,' he promised, and thus began a fruitful period of learning for Nala in this fatefully neglected skill. In gratitude, Nala offered to also cook for the king, which endeared him even more to Rituparna. He began teaching Nala mathematical odds and the finer points of how to apply those to gambling, all of which Nala drank in with barely concealed excitement.

Four years passed this way, and one day a stranger arrived in Ayodhya. Permitted into the royal court, he said, 'O King, I am here to ask a riddle. This question came to me in a dream, and I have wandered around ever since hoping to find an answer. The question is, "Who was the messenger with wings?"'

'What a vague question. How can anyone possibly know.' the king laughed. The messenger respectfully took his leave, but as he left the court, he was accosted by Nala who had hurried after him.

'My answer to your question is a swan,' he said and ran back inside. The messenger asked people nearby who that was and left at once for Vidarbha to tell Damayanti.

When Damayanti heard about Bahuka, she put the second part of her plan in action. Her father sent word to Rituparna inviting him to his daughter Damayanti's second svayamvara since he wanted her to marry again. It was not considered in any way inappropriate those days for a woman to do so. Rituparna accepted at once, for who had not heard of Damayanti's beauty that had maddened even the immortals.

The news was a big shock to Bahuka as he drove Rituparna to Vidarbha. His Damayanti was to marry again? 'How could she!' he thought furiously, but soberly checked himself, thinking, 'She didn't leave you, did she? First you made her homeless, and then you left her in that heartless way alone in the forest. You are an unmanly coward whereas she is a brave woman.'

When Rituparna and Bahuka arrived in Vidarbha, they were lodged according to their rank. Damayanti sent her servants to find Bahuka and bring him to her apartment. She cried out in dismay when Bahuka appeared. But in a flash, the misshapen dwarf disappeared and in his place stood her Nala. Words cannot describe the joy of their reunion. Nala told Damayanti everything and begged her for forgiveness. 'If it was Kali's evil influence, it's not really your fault, and I forgive you,' said Damayanti. 'But do you have a plan now?'

'Damayanti, I have not wasted my time. I went to Rituparna just to learn to gamble. Now wish me luck when I go to challenge Pushkara.'

But first, Nala and Damayanti went together to Rituparna and told him the whole story, apologizing for the deceit. Thankfully, the astonished king was not offended but gave them his blessings instead. He insisted that he would go with Nala to Pushkara to make sure that there was no cheating.

Challenged to play with gold given by Nala's father-in-law as the stake, Pushkara sent an arrogant reply to Nala to come and lose again, for he felt sure he would win. When Nala and Rituparna arrived in Nishada, Pushkara was openly scornful and patronizing. But when the game began, keenly watched by Rituparna, Pushkara realized to his dismay that Nala had changed. His anger made him play badly, whereas Nala was alert and consistently had the upper hand. Pushkara lost finally and tore out in rage. Nala was now the king again. His ministers and subjects welcomed him back with cheers and showers of flower petals.

Rituparna stayed on as Nala's honoured guest for a few days while Nala sent his swiftest charioteer to bring Damayanti and the children back. Several days of public feasts and ceremonies followed, for everyone in Nishada was delighted to have their rightful and just king back and wanted to felicitate him.

But Nala was no longer the old, carefree hero he had been. His loss and grief had changed him forever into a person who weighed risk carefully, who never committed to what he was unsure of doing and who clung fervently, back inside the royal quarters, to his wife and children, made a thousand times more precious after losing them. Damayanti appreciated the change in Nala and could never bring herself to say a cross word to him thereafter.

In this way, Nala and Damayanti finally lived their lives in deep contentment. One day while out hunting in the forest, Nala was stopped on his horse by an ill-looking man with lines of pain and suffering on his face.

'Who are you and what do you want?' said Nala, raising his bow.

'O King, I am Kali, the gandharva. It was I who caused you so much trouble. Karkotaka's poison burns me still. King, I have celestial powers. I would like to offer you a boon and redeem myself. Please make your wish,' said Kali.

Startled, Nala thought for a minute, stirred by unexpected pity. Neither he nor Damayanti had done anything to offend Kali, and yet he had wreaked so much spite and heartbreak on them. But they had done their best to come out of it and were now as safe and happy as anyone could expect.

'There is nothing I would personally like to have, Kali,' said Nala at last. 'But please grant this wish – that anyone who hears our story will not be afflicted unduly by bad luck and bad wishes.'

Kali raised his shrivelled hand in blessing and Nala rode back to his palace with the very last shadow lifted off of him.

15

I Know Everything

What happens when your life is exposed as being hollow? How do you recover from the grief of losing a whole life? This parable, taken from Sri Ramakrishna Paramahamsa, is from the nineteenth century. It comes from the daily life and conversations of the saint, which were recorded by his disciples. The twentieth-century English writer Aldous Huxley called these accounts 'a liberal education in humility, tolerance and suspense of judgment'. Such praise apart, Ramakrishna is loved and cherished by millions in India and abroad. The Ramakrishna Mission have an all-India track record of showing up to help with food, medicine, clothes and tents during calamities and disasters, besides the valuable long-term services to society that they have provided for over a century in health and education through their clinics and schools. This modern retelling picks up on the saint's conviction that to be successful, we need to be grounded in several realities – physical, moral and spiritual.

Hari Narayan was a greatly learned young scholar. His wife had died of an illness some time back, and he did not know how to bring up his five-year-old daughter, Ruma. He missed his wife in a vague way. More particularly, he missed her when it came to a tidy house, washed clothes and fresh and hot food. Being a man, he had not been expected to help in the housework or look after their daughter. Hari Narayan and his wife had been whole planets apart intellectually, for she had been illiterate, while he was a scholar. But he missed her services and felt unable to cope. Having no parents of his own or married siblings, he finally decided to take his daughter to his wife's parents who lived in a village across the Ganga. Since he stayed in a small, rented lodging, he settled his accounts for good when he left, for he meant to take a holiday for a few weeks at his in-laws' home and travel after that to places of pilgrimage.

It was the onset of monsoon, and the sky was dark and overcast when Hari Narayan and Ruma boarded a boat to take them across the river. They found themselves some good seats on the benches along the sides and sailed off. Hari Narayan looked around him and finding nobody of note, began to talk to the passenger next to him. He was a tall, broad-shouldered man and looked to be a cultivator. Hari Narayan looked at him condescendingly and asked, 'So have you read the Vedanta?'

'No sir, I have not,' said the man with a smile.

'Really? What about the Samkhya?'

'And what may that be, sir?'

'My good fellow, it is philosophy. But surely you know the Patanjala?'

'I don't have the faintest idea, sir.'

'You poor fellow. You don't know anything. I have spent my life in study, and I know these books backwards.'

'I congratulate you on your learning, sir.'

Meanwhile, storm clouds had gathered, and a fierce wind began to blow. The water rose higher and rocked the boat dangerously. The boatmen tried their best to ride the wind but the mast broke, and the boat tilted heavily to one side, throwing the passengers here and there. Finally, the captain called out, 'Save yourselves! The boat is going under!'

People began jumping into the river in terror. Hari Narayan's daughter clung to him in fear.

'I'm leaving now. Can you swim?' asked the cultivator, preparing to jump.

'No, I cannot,' stuttered Hari Narayan. The boat lurched violently just then, sending them all into the raging river. Hari Narayan struggled in the water, unable to save himself or Ruma, who went under almost at once.

'Ruma! Ruma!' called Hari Narayan in horror, kicking his arms and legs helplessly.

Suddenly, there was a strong hand on his shoulder, and he felt himself being towed towards the riverbank. It was the cultivator, who had seen him drowning and saved him.

Hari Narayan felt small and wretched. His daughter was dead, and he owed his life to the very man he had patronized and been so rude to. Shock, shame and gratitude warred in his heart. He folded his hands before his saviour, tears pouring down his face.

'I don't know how to thank you,' he managed to say in a low voice.

'I'm sorry about your daughter.'

'Why did you risk your life to save me when I was so rude to you?'

'We are all in the river of life together. I don't know the scriptures, but I know how to swim. I just did my duty,' said the cultivator, wringing out his wet clothes.

Hari Narayan was stunned by this reply. This was a philosophy of life indeed, a practical one based on right conduct or dharma. He felt even smaller and also wondered what he would do now.

'What will you do now, sir?' asked the cultivator as though reading Hari Narayan's mind.

Hari Narayan's shoulders sagged in defeat.

'I don't know,' he admitted sadly. 'I have no family left, nor do I have a home or a job. I taught a little at scripture school, but I don't really have an occupation. My parents left me a little money so I spent my time studying.'

'Book learning has not helped you now, sir, if you don't

mind me saying. Come back with me to my village and learn a few survival skills. You will feel stronger for it,' invited the cultivator.

'What is your name, my friend?' asked Hari Narayan.

'Manik,' said the man, and Hari Narayan accepted his kind invitation, deciding to visit his in-laws later at some point to tell them the sad news of Ruma's death.

~

Six months of strenuous village life sweated all the ghee and sugar off Hari Narayan's city bones. Manik took him every day to the river and taught him how to swim. Soon, Hari Narayan grew unafraid of water and rejoiced in confidently stretching his limbs. He thought sadly of Ruma. 'Ah, little one, I failed you. What business had I to live by the Ganga and never learn to swim? If only I had known then.'

A new, penitent tenderness bloomed in his hitherto self-absorbed heart.

'Child, forgive me. Wife, forgive me. I took you both for granted. I did not really love you. Now you are both lost to me forever, and so I cannot even make up for it.' Such reproachful thoughts haunted Hari Narayan's evenings and nights. Sometimes, he had to excuse himself and walk outside, gazing mindlessly at the night sky to shed his tears alone.

He noticed that Manik did not leave him alone even for an hour by day. 'He is trying to keep me busy,' realized Hari

Narayan with grateful incredulity. How kind of Manik and his mother. Hari Narayan felt smaller than ever and grieved even more pitifully that he had lost his opportunity to be a good householder.

Meanwhile, he found that he was making up for it willy-nilly under Manik's tutelage. He learned to milk cows, to drive cattle, mend holes in the thatch, and even learnt how to cook from Manik's mother. Manik was offended when Hari Narayan offered him the pouch of money that had survived the boat wreck and was tied around his waist.

'It is enough that you came home with me. I felt bad about your child and wanted to help you. Don't reduce it to money,' he said.

'But my food ...' faltered Hari Narayan.

'You don't see us going short, do you? There's enough for another mouth, don't worry,' said Manik, appeased.

'I have learnt many things here. But I feel the need to learn a hands-on skill of my own,' said Hari Narayan hesitantly, voicing a wish that had taken root at Manik's home and had slowly been growing.

'What do you feel like learning?'

'I want a skill that requires one to sit and needs concentration. Something I can recite my slokas to as I work, for it won't do to forget everything I've learnt.'

'Would you like to make fine reed mats? My mother could teach you; she is quite artistic,' offered Manik.

'Yes, that would suit me, I think. Let's ask her now.'

Hari Narayan was very happy with mat-making. He

went with Manik's mother to the haat, or weekly market, and learnt to choose fine, thin reeds that would make soft, silky mats.

He learnt to cut the reeds to the right size and weave plain mats at first before he embarked on patterns. Manik's mother was a patient teacher, and Hari Narayan proved quite adept at this new skill. The number of mats that he wove and rolled up grew steadily in a corner.

One day, Manik suggested that Hari Narayan should sell his mats in the town some distance away where a big haat was being held. They set off in high spirits in the bullock cart as if going to a picnic or a fair.

They set up their wares in a good place in the haat, and soon Hari Narayan found that he was doing roaring business. People exclaimed at the finesse and beauty of his mats and seeing value for their money, paid the asking price without the customary bargaining. Hari Narayan had woven the word 'Ruma' into some mats with an artistic flourish, and several women of that name cried out delightedly and snapped them up. Others began to place orders for their names to be woven into mats and Hari Narayan had to write it all down.

A couple of scholars stopped to look and one of them exclaimed in horror.

'Hari Narayan! It is you, isn't it? What are you doing selling mats in the bazaar? Is this a penance?'

'This is my own work and I'm proud of it,' said Hari Narayan unperturbed. 'Meet my friend, Manik. He saved me from drowning.'

The scholars demanded to know the details, and Manik stepped forward at that.

'You are welcome to return with us to my village and hear about it with the evening meal,' he said hospitably.

Hari Narayan looked affectionately at him. Generous as ever, he thought and echoed the invitation.

But the scholars were leaving next morning and invited Hari Narayan and Manik instead to come after closing business to the local Kali temple where they were staying.

The last mat was sold in the afternoon, and they retreated to the Kali temple where the scholars waited. Several people had gathered to hear the tale, including the head priest.

When Hari Narayan told them the whole story, his listeners shook their heads in sympathy.

'You have changed, Hari Narayan,' said the scholars at last. 'You were quite vain, you know. We used to laugh about it. But now you are full of understanding.'

'I learnt more than mat-making and farm work,' said Hari Narayan, his voice breaking with emotion. 'My friend Manik's generosity saved my life, and living with him has helped me deal somewhat with my sorrow. I saw that book learning is good but of no use as mere theory without life skills. But more than that, I saw that we are all in this life together. We sink or swim together. The message of the scriptures actually makes more sense to me now, that we are an interdependent race and equal in our struggle to get through life. How else may we realize the indwelling God that we are all part of, except by helping each other and being useful in some way?'

'You could do more than mat-making,' said the head priest at that. 'Come once a week to the temple to give a public discourse from scripture. Teach a little at our local pathashala. This way your years of scholarship won't be wasted either. You will receive a fee, naturally.'

Everyone exclaimed that it was an excellent idea and nodded approvingly. Hari Narayan looked at Manik, who smiled warmly.

'Do it, brother,' he said, and Hari Narayan gratefully accepted.

He went home with Manik, thanking God for the gradual turnaround in his life. 'I was too useless to save either Ruma or myself. But I was given the chance to live on and make something of my life,' he thought soberly. 'I won't drown now.'

16

Not Even a Pan

Some calamities are like the sky falling on our heads for no discernible fault of ours. Other troubles are self-created by our own errors. This tale is taken from several parables of Sri Ramakrishna Paramahamsa. To err is human. But must a person suffer forever because of a mistake? Ramakrishna taught that it was not so. Many of his recorded parables are extremely short in length but vast and deep in content. It is up to the listener or reader to make sense of them and find the possibilities of recovery after a painful loss.

Haren was the poor relative of a rich landlord in Bengal. The landlord lived in Calcutta in a fine town house with carriages and horses at the back and an inner courtyard with roses, oleanders and English flowers growing in tubs and pots. He had a wife and two daughters. His wife was as fond of society as he was, and they lived a busy life with parties, soirees and picnics. Haren's mother, a distant cousin of the landlord's, brought him to town to ask the landlord for a job for Haren. Perhaps he could be a clerk at one of the landlord's warehouses?

The landlord had a house and estate deep in the countryside. His old steward had recently died, and he needed a replacement. He offered Haren the job and said he could stay with him in Calcutta for a month to learn accounts from his munshi.

This proved to be Haren's undoing. The glittering life he saw around him in Calcutta filled him with want. He took to closely observing the landlord when he had the chance, to learn how rich folk spoke and behaved. He learnt about the fine things in the Calcutta mansion from the house servants. There was so much to look at and learn about, including silk curtains, blue-and-white Chinese jars, marble-topped tables, vases of flowers, silver and porcelain.

He was too shy, and too lowly, to speak to the landlord's family, staying as he did in the servants' quarters beyond the back courtyard. But he observed how society men behaved with the ladies and made a note of the courtesies and flourishes.

Haren wanted to be their equal but knew that he could not be. He was sent off to the estate when his month was up, his head full of imaginings. All Haren owned, apart from two sets of dhotis and kurtas, was a small battered trunk with some pots and pans in it. His mother had assembled them for him with some difficulty.

Haren found that he had a free hand at the estate. The other servants – the sweeper, the gardener and the cowherd – were few and even lowlier than him. He chose a comfortable room, unpacked his shabby, dented utensils in the kitchen and thoroughly explored the house.

Finding a cupboard open, he discovered knotted bundles of the landlord's clothes and helped himself to a number of fine kurtas, dhotis and shawls. He even found Russian-leather slippers that fit. There was an ebony walking stick with strange figures carved on the head. Haren decided it would make a fine accessory to stroll around with in the garden.

His neighbours saw him out and about, and Haren told them he was the landlord's nephew and the new owner of the estate. If a traveller stopped for a glass of water, Haren offered him buttermilk. 'Whose house is this?' they would ask, and Haren would say, 'It's mine. This house and the gardens, they're all mine.'

This continued for some months until the fateful day that Haren decided to catch a fish. There was a fine, large earthen pond on the estate well stocked with pabda catfish. Haren was partial to pabda macher jhol, a spicy fish curry, and his mouth watered for it. He carefully laid out all the spices he would require, ground the spice paste and stepped out to catch himself a fish. He took along the ebony cane with a flap of cloth tied on it to bring the fish home.

Stepping into the pond, Haren had just taken hold of a slippery pabda when he heard the sound of carriage wheels. It was the landlord who straightaway spotted Haren dressed in his clothes, catching his fish in his pond.

The landlord leapt out of the carriage in fury.

'You thief!' he shouted. 'I was coming to give you your wages. Now take this!'

He grabbed the ebony cane, hauled Haren roughly out of the pond and began thrashing him scientifically. He drove him out of the gates and slammed them shut.

That was it. Haren was out on the road without his wages, his spare dhoti and even his dented pots and pans, his only possessions.

Haren wept in shame and humiliation as he stumbled along the road. 'It was just a fish! Why did he kick me out so cruelly?' he sobbed, still refusing to see the point.

After a while, he stopped at a small roadside pavilion made by some charitable soul for travellers to rest in or shelter from the rain. An old sadhu sat there in monumental stillness. But his eyes were lively and bright as he took in Haren's distraught face. Haren saluted him automatically and sat down in a morose heap.

'What is the matter, son?' said the sadhu after some time.

'Venerable sir, I am in big trouble,' blurted Haren, and with a little coaxing, poured out his sorry tale.

The sadhu did not say anything at first. After a while, he said gently, 'Let me tell you a story.'

'Once, an ant discovered a heap of sugar. Just one grain

filled its stomach. Carrying another grain, it set off towards its anthill. It thought triumphantly, "Next time, I will take away the whole sugar hill."' Son, this is how ignorant minds think. They want everything they see. Whereas the real treasures are three. First, self-respect. It does not come from material things but from honourable conduct and lack of greed. The second treasure is honest effort. Work hard to make something of yourself. You will not be left without even a pan. Third, seek and find God in everything and everyone around you. When you realize you are part of a whole, you will not feel cheated and denied by things on the surface.'

Haren looked on, only half comprehending, so the old sadhu told him another story.

'There was a sadhu once who lived above the naubat khana, or music room, of the temple at Dakshineshwar. He never spoke to anyone and spent all his time meditating on God. One day a big, black cloud suddenly darkened the sky. But after a few minutes, a strong wind blew away the cloud. The holy man came out of his room and began to sing and dance on the veranda.'

When asked about this unusual merriment, the sadhu laughed and said, 'Such is Maya, the illusion that covers life. First there is a clear sky, then there is a dark cloud and soon it's a clear sky again, just as before.'

Haren understood this better. 'So my misfortune is just a passing cloud, isn't it?' he asked.

'Indeed it is, if you provide the strong wind of effort to

blow it away,' said the old sadhu. 'If you would care to take my advice, go back to Calcutta. Go to the Dakshineshwar temple and tell them you met me. Tell them the truth as you told me and say that you want honest employment. Perhaps they can help you.'

Haren thanked the old sadhu but was not immediately consoled. His pain and humiliation were so intense after his traumatic beating and expulsion that the only thing he felt capable of doing was to go home and lick his wounds. He made his way back to his village, hitching rides now and then on passing carts, brooding over the stories the sadhu had told him.

Back home, his mother's reaction pained him immensely. 'Is this what I brought you up to do? We can never show our face to them again,' she wailed when she heard the whole story. The next few months were very difficult and lonely for Haren, who was too ashamed to step out freely. His biggest grief was over the loss of his self-respect and honour.

'I was a fool,' he thought bitterly. 'Why did I lay my greedy hands on what was not mine to take? I cannot blame him for his reaction. I would have been angry, too, in his place. I am left with nothing, not even my old pots and pans, the only things that were mine.'

A whole year passed in this miserable fashion. Haren's mother grew increasingly annoyed over her son's lassitude. One day, she lost her temper and spoke bluntly to him.

'You have wasted enough time at home doing nothing. I helped you in the only way I could. I cannot do more. We are poor and it is shameful that a grown-up son sits idling at home. Now go out and find yourself a job.'

Haren was shocked. His own mother was casting him out. He stumbled out of the house, weeping, and went to sit under the neem tree outside.

A green twig had fallen down, and Haren absently plucked a leaf and chewed it. Its bitter taste made him grimace. This is what truth tastes like, he thought. But just as the neem could cure ills, so could truth.

He had thought long and hard about the old sadhu's stories, and now he remembered his friendly advice. Perhaps it was not too late? He would go to Calcutta and find out. Haren's mother approved of his plan and blessed him. He set out on the road to Calcutta with only a few coppers, greatly fearing more rejection and humiliation. 'I will drown myself in the Ganga if I am insulted again,' he thought wildly and rebuked himself the next instant for being cowardly.

It took a few days for Haren to reach Calcutta, and he stopped only to wash his face and smooth down his clothes and hair before asking the way to the Dakshineshwar temple.

Entering the big, beautiful temple daunted him at first, but he politely asked for the head priest and was taken to see him.

When he heard Haren's unvarnished account of everything that had happened, the head priest took some time to reply.

'Jagat Seth is a great patron of the temple and likes to give people a helping hand,' he said at last. 'Go to the temple kitchen now and be fed. You can stay the night here. We will see tomorrow about Jagat Seth.'

In what seemed like no time at all, Haren, to his unbounded relief, found a job as a clerk in one of Jagat Seth's many warehouses by the Ganga. Never again did he take what was not his and worked very sincerely to keep the second chance that he had been given. Several years of hard work and irreproachable conduct paid off, and Haren found himself as secure as he could be. His mother came down to Calcutta to keep house for him, and by and by, began to talk of finding him a bride. But Haren was, strangely, reluctant. The story of the old sadhu who danced and sang about the passing cloud was burned in his brain.

'We'll see, Mother. I'm not ready yet,' he said, and went off cheerfully to work, profoundly grateful to be employed and be respectable again after his terrible shame.

17

The Secret

Trailanga (Telugu) Swami's life was turned upside down as a little boy. In one sense, he never got over it. But he did try very hard in a way that worked for him and became a legend in his lifetime. No one seems to quite agree on the precise dates, but they do say he was born in Andhra Pradesh in the seventeenth century and lived for a very long time, over two hundred and eighty years. This longevity is attributed to his extraordinary yogic powers. The swami is a household name in Bengal. There is even a popular 1960 Bengali film based on his life story. Sri Ramakrishna Paramahamsa reportedly met him in Benaras in the nineteenth century and described him as 'the walking Shiva of Kashi'. Renowned historian Sir Jadunath Sarkar wrote a book on Trailanga Swami's ascetic order titled *A History of Dasnami Naga Sanyasis*.

Trailanga Swami is still a legend in Benaras, where he is said to have spent one hundred and fifty years and died on a Monday – the day of the week sacred to Shiva – on 26 December 1887. The folklore around him, as a yogi who defied the five elements and the laws of gravity, drank poison without any ill-effects and other such superhuman feat, is monumental. But of special interest is his all-too-human journey from loss and grief to emotional stability, to a whole new 'otherness'.

Narasimha and Vidyavati doted on their little son, Shivaram. Life was peaceful and satisfactory in their little home, deep in the Telugu country. Narasimha was named after the ferocious man-lion avatar of Lord Vishnu, beloved of the Telugu lands. The Telugu people had definite tastes, be it in their favourite, fierce avatar of Narasimha; in imperious, strong-willed heroines like Satyabhama, the warrior queen consort of Lord Krishna; or in their spicy food flavoured with red-hot chillies. But Shivaram's father, despite his fierce name, was gentle and scholarly, often lost in his studies.

Vidyavati was a strong personality who did not put up with any nonsense from anybody. She was direct in her dealings but also affectionate and kind by nature. Shivaram was his mother's little shadow and had to be to be shooed out to play under the mango trees when Vidyavati was praying or busy with household chores.

One day, when Shivaram was barely five, his father took ill with dysentery and thereafter died. Vidyavati bravely shouldered her responsibility alone as a mother and householder. But little Shivaram went into deep shock. 'I will never see Father again,' he brooded and not knowing how to express his feelings, turned dull and dispirited. He stopped playing the childish little games that had given him so many happy hours. His wooden tops, spinning stick, little clay cart and ball lay discarded in a corner.

'The work of childhood is to play,' thought Vidyavati sadly. 'Let me try to divert him.'

She arranged for Shivaram to stay and study with a local learned man, hoping that the gurukul would steady her son. The teacher and his wife were kind to the fatherless child but Shivaram's heart was not in it. He learnt his lessons unenthusiastically and refused to repeat them at home on visits to Vidyavati.

Many years went by like this, and Shivaram did not recover from his depression. His learning went on but he remained a bereaved little boy at heart, unable to ever fully smile or laugh. He resented it that other boys had all of their family, with everyone in place. But this dull ache could never be expressed, and his sullen, withdrawn air meant that he had no friends at all.

Vidyavati meanwhile succumbed to the strain of years of fatigue and putting on a brave front. She took ill one day and grew weaker and weaker. Shivaram rushed to her bedside when he heard about her ill health.

More than her illness, it was Shivaram's lacklustre attitude that worried Vidyavati. He had flatly refused to get married and was now almost forty. He had stayed on at his gurukul as an assistant to his teacher. He was competent but unenthusiastic and saw neither beauty nor humour in life. As a last resort, she decided to share her secret with him. Telling Shivaram to bathe and return, she took a second bath herself and lit the puja lamp to make the atmosphere auspicious.

'Son, listen carefully,' she said, when Shivaram came back from his bath by the well. 'I am going to tell you a secret. Not even your father knew this, for this is a legacy known only to my family. My grandfather imparted it to me. Son, I will teach you the Kali mantra that he taught me. You have often seen me sitting still for an hour with my eyes closed. You thought I was praying normally. But, in fact, I was meditating on the mantra. It has been the source of my strength. I will teach it you now, and it will be your friend and guide through life. It is my parting gift to you.'

Shivaram memorized it indifferently in his morose frame of mind, not really believing her.

When she died a few weeks later, Shivaram went into an even deeper depression. He neither ate nor drank nor slept. One day, almost as a last resort, he took to reciting the Kali mantra for an hour.

Unnoticed at first but gradually increasing in strength, the mantra took effect on Shivaram's mind and body. Shivaram began to feel physically lighter as the days passed. He fell in love with his breath, of which he became intensely aware because of his meditation on the mantra, and, purely on a whim, he left his gurukul and went to sit by a cremation ground where he was witness to the unceasing play of life and death.

In those stark surroundings, he went into teevra sadhana, or complete meditation, unmoving by day or night. It felt strange at first to sit without moving. His knees hurt in particular and so did his back and neck. Hunger and thirst, so sharp at first, gradually came and went as passing fits. It was rather like how a smoker of hookahs, having given up the habit, might miss smoking very badly from time to time but would wait for the urge to fade. For Shivaram, the hardest thing was to try to overcome sad thoughts of his father and mother, whose loss never left his mind.

Shivaram spent several years like this, determined to find an inner life of peace and stability in place of the fragile outer life of human relationships that he knew ended only in parting and sorrow. His entire childhood and young adulthood had passed by in the shadows because of his depression. Left all alone on earth now, he wanted light and air; he wanted freedom from attachment to earthly bonds. This became his personal goal, but it eluded him. It was thanks to the Kali mantra that he did not kill himself to end his misery. The mantra kept him tethered to an unwilling acceptance of his orphaned state and his earthly life, such as it was.

One day, an elderly naked Naga sadhu happened to walk by with some of his followers. He stopped at the sight of Shivaram, who sensed his presence and opened his eyes. He greeted him with a stiff namaste, his elbows straining as he lifted his arms.

'You are not free yet, son,' observed the sadhu. 'If you were, your joints would be supple and your forehead would be uncreased. Tell me about yourself.'

Out of ingrained respect, Shivaram found his voice, hoarse with disuse, and told the sadhu his story in a few short sentences.

The sadhu looked at him keenly.

'You are ready to take sanyas. I will initiate you, if you like, as a Dasnami sadhu.'

'Please tell me about them, sir,' said Shivaram politely, his interest stirred.

'Son, we go back to the eighth century, when Adi Shankara himself founded ten orders of ascetics. The ten orders are Aranya, Ashrama, Bharati, Giri, Parvata, Puri, Sarasvati, Sagara, Tirtha and Vana. Each order is attached to one of four mathas, or monasteries, also established by Shankara in the northern, southern, eastern and western parts of India. They are Jyoti, or Joshi Matha, in the Himalayas at Badrinath, Shringeri Matha on the banks of the river Tungabhadra in the Kannada lands, Govardhana Matha at Puri by the Eastern Sea and Sharada Matha at Dwarka by the Western Sea.'

'Sir, I have heard that there is a famous matha to the south.'

'Yes indeed, son. I have just been to pay my respects there. It is the Kamakoti Matha in Kanchipuram, the mokshapuri or salvation city in the south country. That is where Shankara returned to after his wanderings and installed a Sri Chakra, or mystic diagram, illuminating the power of the goddess you worship.'

'Sir, which order do you belong to?'

'I am Bhagirathananda Sarasvati. I am a Naga sadhu, belonging to the subdivision that has discarded clothes. I am air-clad or sky-clad, if you prefer.'

'Holy sir, please initiate me and set me fully free,' said Shivaram humbly, deeply impressed by the sadhu's serene face.

'Are you ready to follow the rules of our order, son?'

'What are they, sir?'

'We, Dasnami sanyasis, wear ochre robes and, if we can find one, carry a tiger or leopard skin to sit on like Lord Shiva, our patron god. We wear the Tripundra mark on our foreheads, ideally made with ash from a cremation fire, in three horizontal bands across the forehead and on our arms and chests. We wear and carry necklaces of one hundred and eight rudraksha seeds, which is a power number. We allow our beards to grow and wear our hair loose about our shoulders or else tied in a topknot. We are also called Ekadandi sanyasis because we carry a single bamboo pole as the sanyasi's staff.'

'What else, sir?'

'We congregate at holy events like the Kumbh in the four holy towns when it is held, turn by turn, every twelve years – at Prayagraj by the Triveni, Haridwar by the Ganga, Nashik by the Godavari and Ujjain by the Shipra. We, Naga sadhus, have the right to be the first to enter the holy rivers for a dip. We are fighters, too, when necessary.'

'How can sadhus be fighters, sir?'

'Come now, son, there is a long tradition, as you well know, from the time of Bhrigu Parashuram himself.'

'Sir, I am ready. By your grace and favour, I too will become a Dasnami sadhu.'

The sadhu led Shivaram away from the cremation ground to the river that flowed beyond. They meditated for a few days together, and one day, at the appointed time, Shivaram submerged himself in the waters to ceremonially wash away his life as a layperson. When he neared the bank, the old sadhu held out a sanyasi's staff to ritually pull Shivaram to land and to his new life. He was given a set of ochre robes, a rudraksha necklace and a kamandalu, or brass water-pot. The old sadhu ritually marked him with ash.

Shivaram took the sanyasi's vow to never hurt another living creature if he could help it and prayed to Lord Shiva to guide him always. He also recited the Kali mantra, his best friend, which had kept him alive and had brought the sadhu to him because of his absorption in it.

Shivaram followed Swami Bhagirathananda Sarasvati, pleased with his new monastic name of Ganapathi Sarasvati. Lord Ganesha was as close to his parents as he had been, and he related to that. But Lord Ganesha still had his parents. He, Shivaram, had nobody. The thought continued to prey on him. But his new vow of renunciation marked a slow shift in perception.

As he walked north with the sadhu, who was headed to ancient Prayagraj, Shivaram looked hard at the world passing by. Men, women and children in all their complexity, trouble and joy, now began to seem like actors in a play at the temple during epic week, when wandering troupes performed episodes from the Ramayana, Mahabharata and Bhagavata Purana. He found that he no longer grudged them their joys. Nor did he judge them for leading normal lives, bound to the unswerving wheel of karma.

His life as a sadhu was his chosen normal; that was all. He felt a sudden, great tenderness welling up in his heart for people. He wished them luck and hoped that they would be touched only lightly with sorrow.

Part of his learning with the sadhu was deep yoga. Already entranced by the play of his breathing, Shivaram learnt how to master it completely. The yogic poses that he began to accomplish toned his body and made him feel weightless. No longer did his joints ache when he sat in meditation. Instead, he felt light and free, as though he was floating.

This sensation did not come all at once. It took many months of practice, or sadhana, by which time they reached the holy city of Prayagraj. They bathed daily in the heart-stoppingly beautiful confluence of the Ganga and Yamuna, also offering prayers to the hidden river Sarasvati.

Shivaram found himself a special place on the bank where

he could get a good view of the Triveni, or confluence. It was his chosen spot to meditate on the Kali mantra, and he thanked his mother every day for it. Dreams of the Goddess graced his sleep from time to time and one blissful day, while he sat meditating, he was favoured by a glorious vision of Shiva and Shakti on Mount Kailash. It was so beautiful that Shivaram could feel tears pouring down his face. He had not cried for decades, and it felt very strange but also strangely liberating.

Three years went by like this, with Shivaram growing more and more adept at yoga and deep meditation. One day, although he wore only a loincloth now, he could not bear to wear even that. He tore it off in disgust. Where was the need for anything any more? The long shadow of grief seemed to have faded at last. For the first time since childhood, he felt fully free of mental darkness.

When he went back unclad to the ashram that he stayed in, the old sadhu made no remark. Next day, however, he spoke seriously to Shivaram.

'You are ready now to leave for Kashi. That will be your home. The Ganga will be your sister, Vishalakshi, your mother and Vishvanath, your father.'

'Matacha Parvati Devi, Pitadevo Maheshwaraha, bandhava Shivabhaktascha, Swadesho bhuvana trayam,' said Shivaram, bowing low.

'Well said,' replied the sadhu. 'As Adi Shankara said, "Parvati is my mother, Shiva is my father, my friends are the devout and my home is the three worlds." This means that home is everywhere. Nobody would feel lonely or depressed if they thought that way.'

Shivaram took leave of his kindly preceptor with a full heart. He went to the Triveni for one last look before he took the road to Kashi, silently invoking the Kali mantra to grace the next turn of the wheel. He was ready for anything now.

18

The Call

What if you try hard to overcome loss and sorrow and achieve a good life, but something else takes over and takes it all away? Vallabha (c. 1479–1531) was a South Indian who was born and bred in North India. He was a contemporary of Sri Chaitanya Mahaprabhu of Bengal. Vallabha was inspired to find the Krishna idol called 'Shrinathji' that was first worshipped in Mathura and later installed in Nathdwara, a town by the Banas river in Rajasthan. This image is widely depicted even today in the genre of painting called 'pichwai'.

Vallabha did not support monastic life and asceticism. He believed that the love of Sri Krishna was enough of a spiritual path for householders as well as for ordinary men and women. He described it as an everyday love in which simple, glad thoughts of God served to lead a decent and meaningful life. He was the founder of a school of devotion called Pushti Marga (path of nourishment through God's grace), becoming the founder of Sri Vaishnavism in Rajasthan and Gujarat. He wrote several commentaries on scripture and many devotional verses. His famous poem, the 'Madhurashtakam', is frequently sung and danced to even today.

Lakshman Bhat and Yellamma ran for their lives from Benaras at the news of an impending invasion. They made their way with great difficulty to the relative safety of Champaranya, many miles to the east, where they found refuge in a temple dharamshala. Yellamma, who was pregnant, was traumatized by the fear and hardship of their flight. Her son was born two months early, late at night. He appeared to be dead. Heartbroken, the parents covered the little body to await cremation in the morning.

But Yellamma had a dream in which Sri Krishna appeared to her and told her to pick up the baby. She woke up and took the little corpse in her arms. Miraculously, it kicked and cried. Yellamma and Lakshman Bhat were overjoyed. They decided to call their son 'Vallabha', meaning 'precious' and 'dearly beloved'. Lakshman Bhat found employment as a teacher soon after, and they were able to move into a little house of their own.

In gratitude, Yellamma brought up Vallabha to love Krishna. She sang him baby songs about Krishna, brought him painted mud dollies of a crawling Baby Krishna, and often dressed him up as Krishna in a little yellow dhoti with a peacock feather in his hair.

When he was older, she told him a story about Krishna every day. She took him to the local Krishna temple each week and celebrated Janmashtami, Krishna's birthday in August, as though there was a wedding in the family.

Vallabha learnt to dip his fingertips in white flour paste on Janmashtami and make little 'Krishna footprints' from the front door to the puja room, where a big ball of freshly churned butter awaited Baby Krishna should he choose to drop by.

When he was six years old, he asked his mother excitedly, 'Will he really come to our house?'

'We don't know God's ways,' said his mother, smiling tenderly at the thought. 'But if he comes, he will find a warm welcome.'

Growing up with Krishna, in this fashion, left its mark on Vallabha. He spoke to Krishna all the time in his mind, asking him to help him win a game, to tell his mother to make his favourite sweets and, by and by, to help him memorize his lessons, for he was sent off to a gurukul when he was seven.

Vallabha's bright little mind sang and danced at the gurukul. The most complex passages of scripture proved easy for him. His teachers praised him to the skies, and his little classmates looked up to him. He was saved from getting dreadfully vain and spoilt by the example of Krishna, who had been better than anyone else at studies but, said Yellamma, had been very modest and would quietly help his schoolfellows without showing off.

Vallabha's safe, happy world came crashing down one monsoon when typhoid struck Champaranya and carried off both his parents. As refugees, they had no family in town. What would become of Vallabha now?

After the funeral, Vallabha's teacher took charge of his pet pupil and brought him home to stay. The teacher's wife made Vallabha comfortable in her modest home and spoke kindly to him. But his heart was broken.

'Why did you take my parents away, Krishna?' he wept at first. But then a lucky idea occurred to him. 'I have you still,' he thought and went to wash his tear-stained face. He remembered what his mother often used to say about fleeing Benaras and coming to Champaranya: 'When you think only of problems, you get more problems. When you think of possibilities, you get opportunities. We are safe and happy because we took our chances and refused to sit there meekly waiting for our fate.'

Vallabha missed his parents terribly, especially his mother. But as the weeks passed, Krishna became the central figure in his life, his imaginary mother, father and friend. He set himself to study, 'To make Krishna proud', he vowed to himself. 'I have nobody but you, Krishna. You are my possibility.' Brave words, but the doing was harder than the saying. Memories of his parents haunted him every day, especially when he went to sleep and most painfully on Krishna's birthday, Janmashtami.

Several years passed and Vallabha, despite his inner desolation, made steady progress in his scholarship. Word spread in scholarly circles about the bright young student in Champaranya.

When he was about sixteen, a dazzling invitation came his way to take part in a debate in Vijayanagar, in its capital, Hampi. Vijayanagar was the great kingdom in South India that spread from coast to coast of the Indian peninsula. Hampi was like a world stage in its magnificence. Vallabha enjoyed the journey very much, travelling with his teacher and a group of fellow pupils. They made their way by bullock cart, falling in with other groups of scholars headed to Hampi. Vallabha greatly admired the giant statue of Shiva as Virupaksha at Hampi. It was seated in a yogic pose called 'parayank', with the knees drawn up and bound. 'You are magnificent! But I pine to see Krishna, forever sweet and young,' he told the statue in his mind.

The debate lasted twenty-seven days. Was God the same as man, or were the two different? Vallabha contested that man was part of God but adrift on the ocean of earthly life. He needed to find his way back to God in order to become free and complete. Only God's grace could help him do that.

Vallabha spoke with such conviction and gave so many references from all the schools of philosophy to illustrate his points that he was unanimously declared the winner of the debate. He was given gold by the maund, which was about thirty-seven kilos of it, but he distributed it among the poor, keeping six gold coins with which to decorate Krishna's image at the temple of his childhood.

But the victory felt flat for Vallabha. Why were his parents not there to see him shine? What was he going to do with his life without them? Years and years of study stretched ahead of him that seemed pointless without his mother and father.

'I will go on a pilgrimage first,' he resolved, 'perhaps that will help me find a way.' But he made some rules for himself. First, that he would not wear stitched clothes but only a white dhoti and a white upper cloth. Second, he would walk barefoot during his pilgrimage. Third, he would enter a town or village to see its temples but would not stay there and choose to live on its outskirts instead. He made these rules almost instinctively, to simplify his life and be free of wanting things, for that was not the point of pilgrimage according to him. 'Krishna, it is you I long to see, and I'm going to these holy places to look for you, to sense your presence,' he thought.

Vallabha made three long pilgrimages all over central India and the Deccan. He gave discourses at local temples on the Srimad Bhagavatam, the biography of Sri Krishna composed long ago by Veda Vyasa, especially on chapter ten of the Bhagavatam, which detailed Krishna's early life and boyhood adventures. He earned his food through the customary dakshina, or fees, that his listeners gave him. This helped him buy offerings of flowers and coconuts at the temples he visited and also feed the poor from place to place. He went home to Champaranya between his treks and told his teacher about his wanderings and his impressions of the land and people.

'What a marvellous book it would make if you wrote it down!' exclaimed his teacher, but Vallabha could not be bothered.

'It was a personal journey, and it's enough to have seen these things,' he excused himself. 'What really upset me, though, was to see people bound up in ritual after ritual or leaving home to become ascetics. They seemed unaware that God is with us in our daily life, that we only have to sense him.'

'What can you do about it?' said his teacher.

'I don't know. But even as I wandered from place to place, to Omkareshwar, Maheshwar, Srirangam, Tirupati, Srikakulam and Adikesava at Kanyakumari, I felt Krishna calling me as though he wanted to tell me something. I think I will go to his old home, to Mathura. Surely he will answer me?'

'Can you bear to go to the north, given how your parents had to flee?' asked his teacher doubtfully.

'I'm told that things are more stable now. I must and shall go to Mathura.'

Vallabha slowly made his way north, taking over a month of steady walking to get to Mathura, the city of Krishna's birth. Fortunately, he encountered no dangers on the way and eventually got there. His heart leapt with joy at seeing the

Yamuna. 'Ah, beloved river of Krishna's play! How blessed am I to see you at last,' he thought, and set about finding an ashram to stay in.

With his scholarship and attainments, Vallabha was soon accepted in the religious circles of Mathura. There, his life took an unexpected turn. When asked why he was not married yet, Vallabha replied that he was not inclined to marry. But a senior saint, though celibate himself, told Vallabha to get married at once. He was Sri Vitthalanath, from the holy town of Pandharpur, who had grown attached to Vallabha on a visit to Mathura and got to know him well.

'If you are serious about helping people realize God, you should lead by example,' said the saint earnestly. 'What does a sanyasi, like me, for instance, know about the joys and sufferings of ordinary people? I say this with absolute honesty, out of love for my fellow beings. Teach them the Krishna-love that you carry like a jewel in your heart, which your mother gave you. It will brighten their lives, as it did yours.'

'But I don't know any girls and I have no family to speak for me,' said Vallabha, though convinced by his opinion.

'Leave it to me,' said the old sanyasi, for all the world like a fond matchmaking mamma, and spread the word amongst his followers. Soon, a highly respectable match turned up in the form of Mahakanya, the pretty daughter of a local priest. Vallabha was duly married and settled down with apparent joy. Two sons were born to him and Mahakanya. They named the boys Gopinath and Vitthalanath. Vallabha wished very much that his parents could see his family but as the householder's life with its daily concerns and its calendar highlights took over, he laid his grief aside deep in his heart.

However, his sleep was frequently disturbed by dreams of Krishna calling him. One night, Vallabha dreamt that Krishna called him to the foot of Mount Govardhan. Taking it as a command, he went there next day and prompted by some inner urge, began to dig at the foot of the hill beneath a fine kadamba tree glowing with golden yellow puffball flowers.

Digging hard, he knew not why, he suddenly found a dark, beautiful image of Krishna with his arm raised, the way he had held Mount Govardhan at the age of seven. Vallabha took it back excitedly and had it installed at home. As word spread, many people came to worship the image. Since the Yamuna was called 'Shriji' in Mathura, and the image had been found in Krishna country, Vallabha named the image 'Shrinathji' or Lord of Sri, which also meant Vishnu, the Lord of Lakshmi.

He began to write out his philosophical views. This made for several books that were widely appreciated by scholars. But Vallabha also wanted to convey their content to the common people. His central message, to which his life was witness, was that God – whom he saw as Krishna – existed in every human heart and in the simple round of daily life. Unable to resist, he also composed devotional songs about Krishna that soon caught the popular fancy. 'Madhuram, madhuram, mathuradipatey akhilam madhuram' (Everything about the Lord of Mathura is sweet) went the refrain and many people hummed it as they went about their lives. This was his tribute to his mother who had installed Krishna-love in his heart in the first place and given him beautiful memories of family life, which he refreshed in his new life as a husband and father.

Vallabha was now fifty-two years old and should have been content, but the dreams persisted. 'You have done your work here. Now come to me at Kashi,' said Shrinathji in his sleep. Vallabha tried to ignore this message, for he dreaded the thought of giving up the joys of his family life and going to Benaras, the city his parents had fled in disarray.

But he made a conscious effort to pull himself together. 'I have held you in my heart always, Krishna,' he thought. 'Despite being an orphan, I tried my best to make something of my life, encouraged by thoughts of you. What do I have that I have not received by your grace? If you want me to give it all up now, I will. My heart has always been guided by you. I will and shall go to Kashi.'

Being the all-or-nothing person that he had grown to be, Vallabha decided to take sanyas and become a renunciate, for 'going to Kashi' had many connotations, including 'going away for good', in those days when travel was difficult and dangerous. He bid farewell to his tearful wife and children, blessed them to keep on with his teachings and changed his habitual white clothes for ochre robes. He made his ascetic vows sincerely. Bowing deeply to the image of Shrinathji, he left for Benaras with a light, carefree heart. It was going to be all right, he thought. It was Krishna who had consoled him through his years of loss, called him north to Mathura and bestowed a happy family life on him, revealed himself as Shrinathji and blessed society through him and inspired him to write the works and verses that had brought him renown. Now Krishna had called again, and he was bound to answer.

19

Life Lost and Gained

One of the most popular jatakas in Southeast Asia, retold in modern times as an illustrated story by the Thai king, Rama the Ninth, and also made into an opera, this story tells the tale of Prince Mahajanaka who, driven by his loss, developed the grit and determination to recover his lost rights and later make astonishing life choices. The jataka is vividly illustrated on the walls of Cave One at Ajanta and may be seen even today, although it was painted as long ago as around 200 BCE. The story was apparently told to the bhikkhus by the Buddha himself at the forest retreat of Jetavana, outside the ancient city of Sravasti, capital of the kingdom of Kosala in northern Uttar Pradesh. It is where the Buddha lived for the most part after his renunciation.

Ten-year-old Janaka was pushed to the ground by two rough boys who sat on him and beat him with their fists. He struggled to shake them off and finally succeeded. He kicked them around the playground, and they began to howl aloud in pain.

'What's going on?' shouted an adult walking by, and the boys pointed to Janaka and yelled, 'The widow's son is bullying us.' The adult separated them and sent Janaka home to cries of 'Widow's son! Widow's son!'

Janaka was sick of being called that. He wanted to sort this out once and for all. He ran home to his mother. He and his mother lived in the house of a priest and his wife. His mother called the priest 'brother'. Janaka knew no other home except this in the city of Kalachampa on the shores of the Mahodadhi, the Eastern Sea.

He found his mother at home and planted himself squarely before her. 'Mother, tell me the truth. Who is my father? What is the priest to you?'

'He is my brother, son,' said his mother.

'Why am I teased all the time as the widow's son? Tell me the truth, Mother, or I will run away. I won't live like this.'

Seeing his resolution, his mother sighed and made him sit down.

'It's a long story,' she began. 'Your father, Aritthajanaka, was the king of Mithila. We lived in the royal palace. His brother, Polajanaka, killed him in battle. You were in my womb at that time. To save you, I decided to run away. I packed some gold and jewels in a basket and covered it with straw. I put on my maid's old clothes and poured dust over myself. Thus disguised, I went out unnoticed through the palace gates.

'But once outside, I did not know what to do. I had heard of the city of Kalachampa, sixty leagues away, and wanted to go there to be safe. But I had never been anywhere alone outside and did not know how to get there. As I sat by the road, exhausted already by my condition, an old man with a cart stopped by me and asked how he could help. When I told him I was pregnant and wanted to go to Kalachampa, he promised to take me there. He helped me climb into his cart, and I found there was a mattress in it. There was a cloak at the head of the mattress that he told me to wear and a cake that he gave me to eat. I went to sleep almost at once. That evening, I was woken up by the old man who said we were at the southern gate of Kalachampa.'

'But how did we get here so fast, Father?' I asked, astonished.

'I took the straight road,' he said, and vanished. 'I am convinced it was Sakha, Lord Indra himself, who came to my aid. He looked like a god to me. I walked into town and found an airy public hall to sit in. There, I was noticed by the priest I call brother, who asked me who I was. I told him the entire truth. He was touched by my plight and offered to shelter me in his house. He and his wife looked after me with great love and care. You were born safely to me and when you were old enough, I sent you to the gurukul. We are safe here, my son, thanks to them. Polajanaka would have killed me otherwise, to kill you.'

'You trusted yourself to a strange man like that? Oh, Mother, how brave you were.'

'Son, I was desperate, and my only thought was to save you and bring you safely into the world.'

'So I am really a prince? Mother, one day I will take back my father's kingdom.'

Janaka could not get over this astonishing truth. He burnt with anger against Polajanaka and grieved that he would never know his father.

But he also found that he no longer minded being called the widow's son. Since his mother had pointed out the danger of disclosing his true identity, he merely hugged the thought to himself, treating it like a grown-up secret. He set himself to study hard, to run, wrestle and swim, and the priest found an old soldier to train him in archery and sword-fighting.

'Why do you need to learn these things?' teased the local boys, at which Janaka laughed. 'To beat you up with.'

Enthused by his pupil's skill at swordplay and bows and arrows, the old soldier even took him to a friend who taught him horse riding. Janaka threw himself into learning these princely skills. He was sure he would need them one day. He grew tall, strong and well coordinated, and developed the ability to stay focused without losing his nerve. The fierce little boy had made himself into a close-mouthed, confident person, driven by his loss and anger.

Janaka never stopped thinking about his lost kingdom. One day, when he was sixteen, he decided to take the next step. 'One can't raise an army without money,' he thought. 'I need to earn enough money for that.'

He had a serious talk with his mother about his plans.

'Mother, do you have any money? If not, I will take to trade anyway and earn enough to seize my father's kingdom.'

'Son, take the gold I brought with me. Do not trade.'

'Why not, Mother? What's wrong with being an honest trader? I'll tell you what. I will take half of it and cross the sea to Suvarnabhumi. I have heard it is a rich land. I will earn enough wealth there and come back to win Mithila.'

'Son, the sea is very dangerous. I beg you not to go!'

But Janaka could not be dissuaded and found a ship that would take him to Suvarnabhumi, the golden land.

After just a few days at sea, the ship ran into a violent storm. Planks gave way from its sides and water rushed in. Amid the turmoil, shouting, weeping and praying, Janaka did not panic. He proceeded to fill his stomach with stored wheat cakes and fruits. He covered himself with oil to stay warm in the water. He went up to the mast and held on tightly to it. The ship sank, and many of its passengers were eaten by ferocious fanged fish almost as soon as they fell into the water. But the mast, with Janaka attached to it, was thrown beyond the circle of danger.

Janaka swam and floated alternately for seven whole days. There was no sign of land. He was not sure what would become of him, but he felt he must try, anyway. He refused to give in to despair. The sun burnt his face and the salt water cracked his lips, but he tried his utmost to keep swimming and not go under.

On the seventh day, he suddenly found a fairy being calling to him from the air. He thought at first that he was hallucinating, but the being spoke again.

'O man, how long have you been in the sea?'

'Seven days,' said Janaka faintly.

'There is no land for miles. Why have you kept going when there is no point?'

'At least I won't die feeling bad that I didn't try,' retorted Janaka.

'I like that. Who are you?'

'Prince Janaka of Mithila.'

'I will help you, for I am Manimekhalai, the guardian of seafarers.'

So saying, the goddess swooped down, her delicate golden bracelets jingling musically, and took Janaka in her arms. Thrilling at the divine touch, Janaka closed his eyes and dropped asleep from exhaustion. The goddess carried him to Mithila, where she laid him on his side on a ceremonial slab in the royal park and flew away.

Polajanaka died that very moment in the palace. Left without a king, for Polajanaka had no sons, the ministers decided to fall back on an ancient custom. They sent out the royal chariot, drawn by lotus-white horses, to go around town. Whoever it stopped by, if worthy, would be the new king.

Followed by the ministers and high officials, the horses went all around town without stopping. Finally, they headed into the royal park.

'What's the use of that?' said the general, but the priest said, 'Let them go where they like.'

They soon saw that the horses had stopped by the sleeping form of Janaka. The priest carefully examined the soles of his feet and pronounced that he had royal marks. They woke up Janaka and offered him the crown. When Janaka told them who he really was, they cheered with joy and decided to crown him 'King Mahajanaka', which was his grandfather's name. Janaka sent for his mother and the priest and his wife to witness his coronation. His heart, however, felt strangely cold. He had recovered his father's lost throne, but it could not bring back his father. That grief would never leave him.

The people of Mithila were ecstatic over the return of their rightful king. The jataka says, 'The whole city was in a stir to see him, and they came from different parts with presents. They prepared a great festival in the city, covered the walls of the palace with plastered impressions of their hands, hung perfumes and flower-wreaths, darkened the air as they threw fried grain, flowers, perfumes and incense, and got ready all sorts of food to eat and drink. In order to present offerings to the king they gathered round and stood, bringing food hard and soft, and all kinds of drinks and fruits, while the crowd of the king's ministers sat on one side, on another a group of priests, on another the wealthy merchants and the like, on another the most beautiful dancing girls; people skilled in festive songs sang their cheerful odes with loud voices and hundreds of musical instruments were played.'

Janaka was married shortly after to Sivali, the daughter

of Polajanaka. They were happy enough and soon had a son whom they named Dighavu Kumar.

'None of this would have happened had I not been strong those days in the sea,' thought Janaka with a shudder of relief. His heart felt strangely unquiet, although he had achieved his goal. Why did his father have to die? Why did his mother have to escape to dependency on strangers? And why did have to grow up in disguise? The wrong done to his father weighed incessantly on his mind despite having regained his kingdom.

One day, when not quite thirty years old, Janaka decided to spend a morning in the royal gardens. Followed by his attendants, he entered the garden seated on the royal elephant. Near the gate grew two mango trees. One was laden with ripe fruit while the other had none. Janaka plucked a ripe mango from atop his elephant and found it very sweet and refreshing. 'I will have more on the way back,' he thought, and proceeded to enjoy his round among the fruit trees and scented creepers.

When he returned to the mango trees, Janaka was shocked to see that the fruiting tree was now a pitiful sight. All its fruit was gone, and its branches were battered and broken. The fruitless tree, on the other hand, stood unviolated, green and glorious.

'What happened?' he thundered, and the gardener stepped out, trembling. 'O king, once the people saw that you had plucked a fruit from this tree, they fell on it and plundered it,' he said.

Janaka was moved to the core. 'This world is like the fruiting tree,' he thought with sudden, new sadness. 'It creates its own ruin. Whereas the tree without fruit lives out its days serenely. So too must be the life of an ascetic without worldly bonds.'

Back at the palace, Janaka could not stop thinking about this new realization. He tried to do something practical, meanwhile, to calm his mind. He issued orders that a thousand mango, jamun and shade trees, like the neem and pipal, be planted all over Mithila. He ordered new wells to be dug and water channels and ponds made all over the kingdom, and built five hundred new dharamshalas, or rest houses, for travellers and pilgrims. 'Let them feel they have enough,' he thought.

Although he was satisfied with his good works, he was unable to stop thinking about the fate of the two mango trees and his reaction to it. The feeling of detachment from his royal life grew stronger and stronger until one day, with his customary directness, he decided to act on it.

He called his mother, wife and ministers to a council.

'I am going away with only a begging bowl,' he announced to his shocked listeners. 'Let Queen Sivali bring up Prince Dighavu Kumar to be a good king, with wise advice and good counsel from you all. No, there is no point objecting to it. My mind is made up. I will leave in a month.'

Queen Sivali objected strongly and threw a number of parties where she instructed the dancing girls to distract Janaka and keep him at home. His mother and ministers pleaded earnestly with him not to go. 'This was your dream from childhood – to win back Mithila and be king. You have it all. How can you bear to give it up and go away as a homeless beggar?' wept his mother. When the people of Mithila heard, they thronged the palace gates with loud cries that their king should stay. But Janaka was unmoved. His heart, battered already by his father's fate, was convinced of the pointlessness of wealth and power.

Unmindful of his family's tears, his minsters' dismay or his people's grief, Janaka cut off his long hair and laid aside his crown, jewellery and royal clothes. He put on a robe of ochre and took up the sanyasi's staff. He felt he owed it to himself. He had fought for his self-respect and dignity as a child, practised and studied hard as a youth to develop himself, braved the sea to go to Suvarnabhumi as a trader, kept swimming in the ocean even without hope of land, and thereafter, he had tried to be a good king. He had redeemed his dead father's name without bloodshed, thanks to a welcome bit of luck. But the fate of the two mango trees had profoundly affected him.

'I have done my best and fulfilled all my worldly duties. I never gave up. Now I will go my way and find my soul,' he thought, as he walked out of Mithila towards the holy city of Kashi by the Ganga and was never heard of again, lost in the teeming, separating, dissolving millions of pilgrims who flocked there.

20

Taken at Thirteen

How does a happy little boy deal with being suddenly separated from home and family forever and turned into an ascetic? Sri Chandrasekharendra Saraswati (1894–1994) was the 'Mahaswami of Kanchi', the sixty-eighth Shankaracharya of the ancient Kamakoti Matha, an important religious institution in Kanchipuram in Tamil Nadu. He is a cult figure even today for devotees. His birth star, Anuradha, also called Anusha, is observed every month as a festival in homes across India and around the world by sections of the Indian diaspora. There is a Manimandapam, or memorial temple, dedicated to him in New Jersey, US.

The Mahaswami believed in pluralism and saved the mosque next to his matha from demolition. At the same time, he played a key role in reviving the study of the Vedas, equipping society with properly learned priests to serve homes and temples and teaching the public lost devotional verses. He pioneered the conservation of neglected temples and inspired the building of new ones. Many devotees testify personally to his miracles of healing on YouTube channels and other websites.

While deeply learned, he was simple and accessible and reportedly had a wicked sense of humour. He walked barefoot for miles across India in padayatra. Carnatic music was his grand passion, and the great musicians of the day flocked to him for spiritual insights into the compositions they sang. Pandit Vishnu Digambar Paluskar of the Gandharva Mahavidyalaya came to Kanchipuram and sang North Indian bhajans for him. One of Mahaswami's protégés was M.S. Subbulakshmi, and when she was invited to sing at the UN General Assembly in 1966, he composed the Sanskrit hymn 'Maitrim Bhajata' for her, calling for world peace.

His admirers included a wide swathe of society, across religions, from the very poor to the rich and powerful, from canteen boys to kings. Indira Gandhi, King Constantine II, Princess Irene of Greece, King Juan Carlos and Queen Sophia of Spain were among his fans. But this great sage had a heartbreaking start, an amazing tale of our times.

Swaminathan, or 'Ginni' as he was called at home, meaning 'parrot', was the pet of his family, deep in a small Tamil town in the Madras Presidency. He sang like a bird, topped in Bible class at Mission school to the pride and joy of his Western teachers and was as busy and happy as a normal little boy could be, safe in the love of his parents and siblings. His father, Subrahmanya Iyer, was a school supervisor for the British government and had Ginni and his brothers admitted to the English school to provide them with the best possible modern education available. Ginni's mother, Mahalakshmi, was of distinguished descent. Her long-ago ancestor was the great seventeenth-century musicologist Venkatamakhin, who had mapped Carnatic ragas into the grid called the 72 Melakarta. Another ancestor was Govinda Dikshitar, who had been a minister of the Nayak kings of Thanjavur and had worked very hard to improve the conditions of temples and ghats by the river Kaveri. Music ran in her blood, and she taught Ginni to sing many ragas.

'Listeners should know how to enjoy a song whether it is in a light or weighty raga,' she taught Ginni. 'One should be broad-minded because although tastes may differ, music is everybody's birthright. A song should touch the heart. That is the yardstick, not anything else. Raga Todi has weight while Sindhu Bhairavi is light. Both touch the heart.'

A thought struck Ginni.

'Why do all concerts end with a mangalam?' he asked.

'A mangalam is a blessing,' explained his mother. 'It is in Raag Madhyamavati, which is linked to Raga Kharaharapriya, Sri Rama's favourite raga. It is like a return gift from the musician to the listeners, wishing them well-being and repentance for any sins, knowingly or unknowingly.'

Ginni grew particularly fond of the songs of the eighteenth-century scholar-saint Muthuswamy Dikshitar, whose pseudonym was 'Guru Guha'. This meant 'Kartikeya', the same as Ginni's name, 'Swaminathan'.

'He really describes the gods well,' Ginni told his mother. 'I can almost see them when you sing his songs.'

One day, his schoolteacher came home to ask permission for Ginni to take part in the school's annual production of a Shakespeare play. That year it was *King John*.

'We need your son to play the part of Prince Arthur,' he said.

Ginni's parents did not like the idea at first. 'We don't want him on stage,' they told him. But Ginni spoke up, entreating his parents to let him perform. Unable to say no to their pet, his parents agreed and were persuaded to pay for the costume of leggings, tunic, hat and shoes. Ginni set to work memorizing his lines and learning his cues.

The play went off very well, and Ginni, to his parents' amazement, was the star of the show. Everyone applauded him loudly, and he was given a prize for his role.

'But you had hardly any time to learn your lines,' said his mother as they went home.

'I tried very hard,' said Ginni, giving an involuntary skip.

That year, Ginni's father took the family to a town nearby where the sixty-sixth Shankaracharya of Kanchipuram was on a visit. The family looked up to him as their spiritual guide and went to seek his blessings. The Shankaracharya spoke graciously to them, but Ginni caught his eye.

'Come closer, child,' he said, and Ginni, not shy in the least, came forward at once.

The seer asked Ginni a number of questions about prayer, practice and music. He was greatly surprised by Ginni's confident, precocious answers. Ginni, too, found him deeply interesting. There was a gentle, deep air about the seer that attracted and impressed him very much. A line from Bible class came to mind: 'For it was fitting for us to have such a high priest, holy, innocent, undefiled.'

A few months later, news came that the Shankaracharya had passed away of age. The new Shankaracharya, a very young man, was Swaminathan's cousin.

The family could do nothing about these larger matters and went on with their lives. One day, however, a telegram arrived summoning them to the matha at Kanchipuram. Since Ginni's father had an educational conference to attend at Trichy, he arranged to send his family to Kanchipuram by train. His mother took along idlis wrapped in banana leaves, sweet mountain bananas and buttermilk in a big kooja, or jug with handles. It was an exciting journey for Ginni, who had never gone anywhere by train.

All too soon, they were at Kanchipuram and went to a nearby temple to wash and rest.

An official of the matha was waiting for them with a horse carriage. 'I must take Swaminathan with me at once to the sub-matha at Kalavai thirty kilometres away,' he said, without saying why. 'I have arranged a cart for the rest of you to follow.'

Since he was from the matha, Ginni's mother handed her son over trustingly with a parting hug. The carriage set off and covered a few miles before the official suddenly spoke.

'Do you know why I'm taking you to Kalavai? Your cousin, the new Shankaracharya and his successor, are both dead within a week of each other because of smallpox. You have been chosen as the next Shankaracharya because the sixty-sixth Swami spoke well of you.'

'But I'm only thirteen, and at school. What will my parents say?' said Ginni, shocked.

'We have telegraphed your father for permission. He won't say no. Why should he, when it's such a big honour and he has three other sons? You must follow the rules of a sanyasi's life from now on. You must shave your head, wear ochre, sleep on the ground and never see your family again. A sanyasi has nothing to do with his past life.'

Ginni's head swam. Never see his family again? He felt very small and scared. He sank to his knees on the floor of the carriage and began to say 'Rama, Rama', the only mantra he knew. He stayed on his knees all the way to Kalavai, too frightened to move.

Matters moved swiftly at Kalavai when they got there. A barber shaved off Ginni's black curls. He was made to take a ritual bath and wear an ochre robe. A large bamboo pole, the sanyasi's danda, was given to him to hold. He was not allowed to put it down except during breaks. They made him repeat the sanyasi's vow of renunciation and marked him with holy ash. It was his daily duty, henceforth, they said, to perform the hour-long puja to Lord Shiva, worshipped at the matha as Sri Chandramaulishwara, the Moon-Bearer. Sixty-seven Shankaracharyas before him had done it, stretching back to ancient times.

There, the deed was done. Ginni's parents were rushing to Kalavai and they would wait for that last formality of his father's permission and the last goodbye. He would not be allowed to see them again.

Ginni did everything he was told in a daze, overwhelmed and convinced by the utter seriousness and solemnity of the matha officials. Was he really the chosen one? Stray bits of Bible class floated in his mind. 'Though my father and mother forsake me, the Lord will receive me,' and 'Have I not commanded you? Be strong and courageous. Do not be afraid; do not be discouraged, for the Lord your God will be with you wherever you go.'

'Oh Lord Shiva, O Mother Kamakshi, they say I will be your priest from now on. Help me, save me, protect me!' he thought frantically, his head in a whirl.

His parents arrived the next morning, and Ginni was brought out to them in ochre and ash, looking like Raja Ravi Varma's painting of Adi Shankara. Ginni's mother cried aloud at the sight and stepped forward to hug him, but was held back by her husband.

'He is a sanyasi now. We cannot touch him,' he said sadly.

'How will my precious child handle this hard new life?' wept his mother and everyone looked down in distressed silence. Ginni longed to console her and suddenly found the words.

'Mother, Father!' he said. 'Don't be unhappy. I am sure I have God's blessings. Please give your permission.'

His distraught parents finally agreed and went away with one last yearning look at Ginni. Back home, however, they wept every day for weeks. The other children tried to console them, but they missed Ginni terribly and could not fully believe that he was gone forever. His father sat down one day to read Shakespeare's *King John*, the play in which Ginni had shone just months earlier, and broke down when he came to the lines:

> Grief fills the room up of my absent child,
> Lies in his bed, walks up and down with me,
> Puts on his pretty look, repeats his words,
> Remembers me of his gracious parts,
> Stuffs out his vacant garments with his form.

Meanwhile, Ginni tried hard to hide his tears from his instructors, learned old men who deferred to him as the Shankaracharya, but also spoke sharply if his mind appeared to be wandering. He was taught how to conduct the daily puja and he learnt to do it with patience and purpose. 'It is done to ask Lord Shiva to bless everybody. I must do it properly,' he thought earnestly, and over the next few months learnt to do it so gracefully that old-timers began to say that it reminded them of the sixty-sixth Shankaracharya's fidelity and beauty of worship. But every night, he turned again into a lonely, frightened little boy surrounded by grave, learned older men. What was his mother doing, he wondered miserably and tried very hard not to cry, for his sobs would disgrace him.

They woke him early every morning at four, the sacred hour of the Brahmamuhurtham, when the world was believed to be abuzz with divine energy. After a bath, Ginni was given fruit and milk for breakfast and made to learn Vedic metres, mathematics, astronomy and Sanskrit literature, in addition to Tamil, Telugu and Kannada. He broke off to conduct the daily puja and could spend the late afternoon reading books of his choice. Ginni asked for English books so that he would not forget his schooling. Approved classics were duly bought for him. Ginni was also taught yoga at the deepest level and how to control his body's urges. This took serious practice and Ginni tried his best. He found that yogic breathing helped him to sleep better at night and worked on getting it right to banish his bedtime tears.

The hardest part, Ginni found, was giving up on tasty food. He had spent a lot of his time with his mother while she cooked. He thought longingly of his favourite rava dosas and crisp onion vadas and sighed deeply. He could never eat onion and garlic in his life again; they were forbidden as unhealthy. Delicious food was prepared every day at the matha as prasad and hundreds of pilgrims and the poor were fed daily. But it was unseemly for a sanyasi to gobble, said his instructors. He must not gorge himself, either alone or in public, and learn to avoid sweets and fried food altogether. Ginni tried not to mind when they gave him plain puffed rice and buttermilk as 'sattvik' or pure food. When he was taken out in procession on festival days, they put him in a palanquin. Ginni felt very awkward about being carried around and decided to stop it when he was older.

The matha manager took Ginni to every nook and corner and explained each expenditure to him who could not issue any executive orders until he turned twenty-one but had to learn about the running of the matha in the meantime. Ginni learnt that the palanquin bearers were given money for liquor to make the strain bearable. This made him realize, yet again, that there were rules for him and separate rules for others, and the strictest rules of all fell to his lot.

There were no children to play with at the matha. A Shankaracharya could neither play cricket in the gullies like other little boys did nor run home in the evening to a loving hug and dinner with the family.

Ginni tried hard to find other entertainment that his minders would not consider inappropriate. He spread grain in an open corner of the courtyard to entice the flocks of parrots that swept by the matha. He also played with the sweet newborn calves in the cattle shed and made friends with the temple elephant, Kumbhan, speaking to him often and bringing him bananas.

One day, Kumbhan defied his keeper and refused to leave the pond in which he was enjoying a long, luxurious mud bath. No amount of calling or cajoling worked. The keeper was at his wits' end when someone thought of calling the young swami.

When Ginni arrived at the pond, he merely said, 'Come along now,' and Kumbhan rolled out of the mud and water, and clambered out to follow Ginni to his stables.

Another time when a prime ashram cow went missing, Ginni went searching for her and heard her mooing plaintively in a farmer's cowshed. The farmer explained that the straying cow had eaten up a whole field of his crop. Ginni offered him a sack of rice from the matha as a fair payment which was accepted and brought the cow back.

These small incidents added to Ginni's mystique as the Shankaracharya. He spoke cheerfully to everyone he met, and they in turn told others about the boy seer who had no playmates and so made friends with animals and birds.

Meanwhile, Ginni tried even harder to work on his craving for food. One day, a devotee brought baskets of the finest mangoes from his orchard for Ginni, who noticed Lambadi gypsies moving in colourful bands near the matha.

'Please, share the fruit with those gypsies. They never get to eat such fine mangoes. Give them the fruit with your own hands,' he told the devotee.

Astonished but obedient, the devotee did so and was loudly blessed by the tribe, to his great pleasure, while Ginni retreated to watch from an unobtrusive distance.

This incident gave Ginni another idea. Maternal devotees, longing to bring him nice things to eat, would arrive at the matha with tins of home-made murukkus and laddoos.

'There are young boys at the pathashala who have left home to study. They get only plain fare and must be missing their mothers. These snacks and sweets will be such a treat for them. Please distribute them yourself at the pathashala, the children will be so happy,' he would say. 'Do it to please Mother Kamakshi.'

The mothers did so after their first pang of disappointment that Ginni was sending away their labours of love. At the same time, they felt he was doing a good thing, in which they got to share, and they respected his ascetic indifference to treats. They did not know of his inner struggle to adjust and grow into his new persona.

Ginni had begun to link the big ideas that he was being taught to everyday life, and one day he was struck by a novel notion.

'A typical South Indian meal is served in three main courses,' he thought. 'There's rice with sambar, rice with rasam and rice with curds or buttermilk. Sambar is also known as kuzhambu in Tamil, which also means "to get confused". Don't these three courses seem related to the three gunas of spirituality? The "confusion" of sambar is "tamo guna", the clarified flow of rasam is "rajo guna" and the all-white buttermilk is "sattva guna". Our meal reminds us of our spiritual path. It goes from confused inaction to a clear flow of action and finally to the cool, calm state of realization … but I am too young now to say these things to adults.'

Instead, when he was taken to the Kamakshi temple near the matha, he told the Goddess his thoughts. Anna daanam, or feeding the public, for free was a temple duty, and the Kamakshi temple excelled at it. He thought the Goddess would approve of his analogy. 'One day I will sit here in your temple and share my ideas with people, Mother,' he said in his mind. The goddess glowed back at him in a red sari, her dark face seeming to smile radiantly. Ginni went back to the matha cheered by the beautiful sight.

So many people now thronged the matha to gawk at the boy sanyasi that Ginni's instructors decided to take him away. They chose the hamlet of Mahendramangalam on the banks of the Kaveri, where the matha owned a cottage. It was not easy to reach that village in those days. One had to take a train to a place called Lalapettai and then take a country boat across the Kaveri to reach Mahendramangalam.

Ginni's loneliness increased ten times more in remote Mahendramangalam. There were no young people around, nobody to share a laugh with. Ginni missed his brothers very much, especially in the evenings, although he could now take instruction in peace and quiet. Sometimes his homesickness grew so intense that he thought of running away. But fear of disgrace kept him in place.

Some of the most learned scholars in South India were handpicked to instruct him. When they asked him what else he wished to learn, as though it were not already enough, Ginni said he wanted to learn Marathi and French. So a pandit was brought from Maharashtra and stayed with Ginni for three years. A French teacher came up from Pondicherry and in addition to all the English books he read, Ginni gradually discovered the pleasures of reading Montaigne, Dumas, Maupassant and even Baudelaire, sitting on the dry bed of the Kaveri in spring or leaning against a shady tree.

A music teacher was also engaged, for music was considered part of devotion and a key religious activity. Ginni wished his mother could hear him as his voice broke and he found his new voice.

But a great solace was at hand with the river Kaveri. Ginni learnt to swim and could not bear to leave the water. He became a strong swimmer, and when his teachers couldn't find him on land, they were sure to find him in the water. Ginni was also permitted to go on walks and took to exploring the lush green countryside. He would walk for hours on end after the daily puja was done, which made his legs strong. He saw many beautiful ruined temples, which pained him deeply. 'One day I will fix them,' he vowed.

His growing sense of physical well-being deserted Ginni the night he had an agonizing toothache. His instructors made light of it, and Ginni, only fourteen, was told to bear it stoically. But the wife of his head teacher took pity on the huddled little form. 'He's only a boy still,' she thought, and smuggled him a clove from the kitchen to keep on the afflicted tooth. Clove oil was good for toothache, and the pain gradually eased.

One day, Ginni was given a camera as a scholastic reward for mastering Panini's grammar. He took it everywhere he went, to the sand patches in the Kaveri, to mouldering temples and fine temples alike. He shot scenes of picturesque places and village life and played with light and shade and composition. The local people were startled to see a young sanyasi swimming or taking pictures, but Ginni smiled such a friendly gap-toothed smile at them that they could only smile back and salute his ochre robes. Ginni wished very much that he had a picture of his mother and father to look at sometimes.

His heart ached every time he thought of his parents. How they would have delighted in all the new things he was learning, he thought. The pain would pass after a bit and each time he told himself sternly, 'I am a sanyasi now. I am not allowed to miss my family,' and threw himself into the next activity.

But thoughts of his parents, particularly his mother, would not leave him. He prayed to Kamakshi at Kanchipuram to find him a solution and tried to talk himself out of it.

'We try to hide our faults before others and to show off only our merits,' he thought. 'Sometimes we even cry over our faults. But what's the use of merely weeping? Instead, we should pray to God to give us strength to resist our bad and weak thoughts.' These stern self-appraisals helped him feel better for a while, until the next cycle of yearning and loss arrived to eat at him.

One day, when Ginni was sixteen, a Carnatic singer arrived at Mahendramangalam with his accompanists – a violinist and a mridangam player. They were touring the Kaveri delta and wished to have a glimpse of the young Shankaracharya.

When they began to sing that evening, Ginni had no need to make requests. The singer seemed to know instinctively which songs he liked. After two glorious hours, he slid into the alaap, or exposition, of Raga Madhyamavati. Ginni wondered which song was coming.

'Vinayakuni valeno brovave', sang the musician in Telugu, meaning 'Look on me as you look on your son, Vinayaka.' It was a song addressed by the saint-composer Thyagaraja to Goddess Kamakshi at Kanchipuram. The musician took it slowly in a magnificent, layered build-up to impart the full effect of the plangent notes of Madhyamavati. When he came to the line 'Anatha rakshaki Sri Kamakshi', meaning 'O Kamakshi, protector of orphans', he sang it several times with heartfelt yearning in his voice. As the beautiful words and music seeped into him, Ginni suddenly felt light-headed with the joy of realization.

'I do have a mother,' he thought happily. 'O Mother Kamakshi at Kanchipuram, I will come back to you soon. You have been patient with me, have you not? But I was only thirteen when they took me. I have tried my best to accept my fate and grow up. You know I have. I have studied hard, swum, walked, eaten less and practised yoga every day. I concentrate totally on my daily puja. But I still felt like a little boy. I don't any more, Mother. I have duties ahead of me and you must help me.'

Pleased and satisfied with his thoughts, Ginni sat at ease to hear the singer finish the song. He was no longer 'Ginni' in his mind as he had been until now. He was

Chandrasekharendra Saraswati, a sadhu, and also the head of a matha. His God-given task was to serve society. With Kamakshi's blessings, he resolved that he would do both as long as he lived.

Acknowledgements

I thank my editor, Chiki Sarkar, very much for this book. Any inadvertent errors are mine alone, for which I ask pardon. Do tell me what you think of these stories at jltyouknow@gmail.com.

A Note on the Author

Renuka Narayanan writes on religion and culture. She was Editor, Religion, Arts and Culture for the *Indian Express* and *Hindustan Times* and the start-up Director of the Indian Cultural Centre, Embassy of India, Thailand. She is the author of several books including *What Our Gurus Taught Us*.

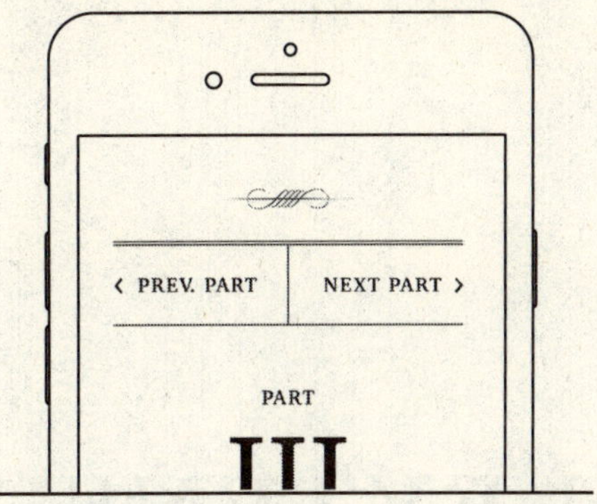

Beautiful Typography

The quality of print transferred to your mobile. Forget ugly PDFs.

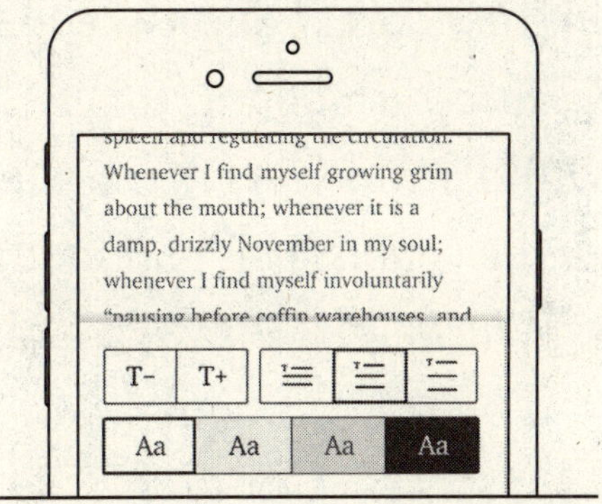

Customizable Reading

Read in the font size, spacing and background of your liking.

AN EXTENSIVE LIBRARY

Including fresh, new, original Juggernaut books from the likes of Sunny Leone, Praveen Swami, Husain Haqqani, Umera Ahmed, Rujuta Diwekar and lots more. Plus, books from partner publishers and loads of free classics. Whichever genre you like, there's a book waiting for you.

juggernaut.in

DON'T JUST READ; INTERACT

We're changing the reading experience from passive to active.

Ask authors questions

Get all your answers from the horse's mouth. Juggernaut authors actually reply to every question they can.

Rate and review

Let everyone know of your favourite reads or critique the finer points of a book – you will be heard in a community of like-minded readers.

Gift books to friends

For a book-lover, there's no nicer gift than a book personally picked. You can even do it anonymously if you like.

Enjoy new book formats

Discover serials released in parts over time, picture books including comics, and story-bundles at discounted rates. And coming soon, audiobooks.

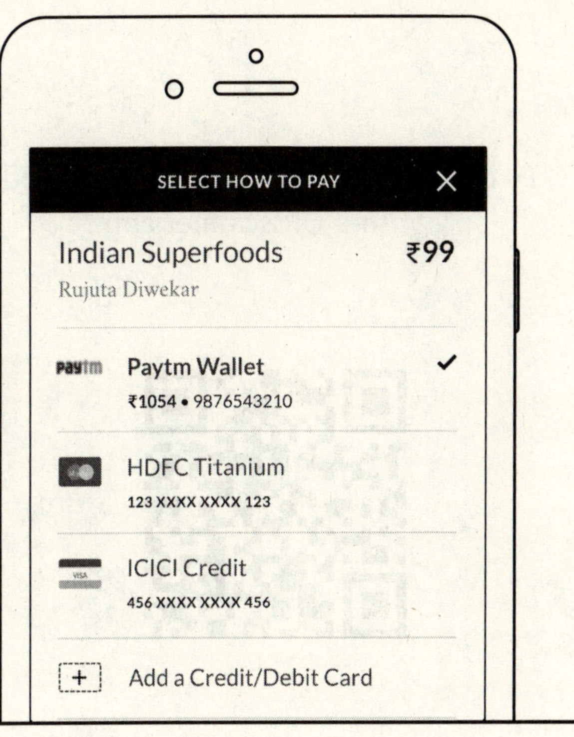

Paytm Wallet, Cards & Apple Payments

On Android, just add a Paytm Wallet once and buy any book with one tap. On iOS, pay with one tap with your iTunes-linked debit/credit card.

To download the app scan the QR Code
with a QR scanner app